A Cat's Tale

Michael Smith

A CAT'S TALE

FAST BOOKS

for Alfred

Cover painting by Michele Hawley,
collection of Hinrich and Laurel Müller.
Author photo by Kim Reierson,
Santa Barbara Independent.

Fast Books are edited and published by
Michael Smith
P. O. Box 1268, Silverton, OR 97381

ISBN 978-0-9982793-7-4

History is not a piece of crockery dredged up from the Titanic; it is, first, the shipwreck, then a piece of writing.

Jacques Barzun
The Culture We Deserve

A Cat's Tale

Chapter 1

Little did I know what I was getting into when I let her pick me up and carry me away. Not that I had any choice. I was young. I had never been away from home. I am a dependent creature. I admit it.

Everything had already been changing so when several of us were tossed into a box and tippily carried off, it was just one more unexpected development. Suddenly it was cold. We snuggled together in the corner as best we could, purring to keep warm. Then clickety clack we were on a train. There were holes in the box but I didn't want to look.

When we were finally put down and the top of the box was folded back, we found ourselves in a big bright room with a cluster of faces looking down at us saying, "Oh, aren't they cute!" Several hands came down at us and we prepared to surrender, but someone said, "No, not now. Wait till we have a break."

"Put them over here where it's warm. Do they have water?"

"I'll get some."

There was much shuffling around. Someone

put a glass bowl full of water on the floor of the box. We wandered over to it one by one, pretending we didn't care. It wasn't very good. Why didn't they give us some food?

Things settled down until it was so quiet I thought everybody had gone so I crept over to one of the holes and looked out. What I saw was a naked man standing motionless on a platform surrounded at a distance by humans at easels making drawings of him in black and white and color. The vibe was extremely mellow. I wanted to draw a picture of them drawing pictures. Ha ha. And the naked man was interesting, not quite what I expected. Hairless, mostly.

We played a little, nervous as we were, and took a nap. They were hanging over us again when I woke up, reaching down and touching us with their fingers and rubbing our fur and scooping us up in their hands, me last. I liked being picked up. I snuggled and wriggled and found myself lifted right up against a soft warm cheek with a voice humming very softly, practically breathing my breath.

"Can I have this one?" it said.

"Yes, yes. I want them all to find homes. They are very sweet but we have enough cats."

"Is it a boy or a girl?" the voice said, turning me upside down and pushing my back legs apart. "I can't tell."

"I think it's a boy, but it's hard to be sure when they're so little, there's not much difference."

"I think it's a boy." I wasn't sure what they were talking about. Something to do with the litter box? Well, everything would become clear, or not.

"One more pose," someone said.

The soft hands put me back down in the box. "Now don't let anyone else take him," she said.

"They won't. He's too funny looking."

"I find him quite remarkable."

"Yes, he's very nice, I played with him a lot. He is very friendly. His mommy is the best cat in the world."

They went back to their art and then it was time to go. The rest of the litter were taken away, looking around with big eyes and mewing as they were carried off. Someone took the box too but I was perfectly comfortable in the hands of my person, who had a coat and hat on now and was rather clumsily wrapping me up in the end of her scarf.

"I have to walk home," she said, "and it's

snowing. Will he be all right? I don't want him to get cold."

"He'll be all right if you're all right."

"Help me get this shoulder bag on," she said. "Thank you for this beautiful creature. He's for my boyfriend. He needs a cat. See you next week." With that she tucked me inside the front of her puffy coat and we went out into the storm. It was snowing hard, snow blowing in swirls and eddies under the streetlights, traffic sparse and hushed on the white pavement. She leaned into the wind as if climbing a hill, holding me close and hurrying along. I liked it very much.

•

"I brought you a present," she said when we were inside again.

"What is it?" said a deeper voice.

She extracted me from her bosom, untangled me from her scarf, and put me into his hands. He was startled and almost dropped me. This was a person unaccustomed to holding a living animal.

"Good heavens."

"Isn't he adorable?"

"I'm not sure I want a kitten."

"Yes you do. You will love it."

"We can't have a pet. It's in the lease. Mrs.

4

Johnson was definite. She doesn't even like having you here."

"She likes me."

"She is polite, but she would like it better if you were not here."

"She doesn't have to know about him."

"I don't think that's fair. I like Mrs. Johnson. It's her house, after all."

Looking around I saw a softly lit white room with a mirror over the mantle and an odd-looking piece of furniture I later learned was a harpsichord. While they were talking she had taken her coat off and hung it up in a closet.

Carrying me precariously he followed her through a little hallway into a purple room with a big low bed. He put me on the bed and they both sat down and looked at me. "I can't take him back," she said. "I promised." Standing up on the soft surface I stretched my back and neck and tried to make sense of my surroundings. I wobbled across to look over the edge and lost my balance and started to fall; he caught me and put me back in the middle of the bed. "How can you resist?" she said.

"I like the way he looks," he said. "He's so vivid." I was different from the others; they were all speckly gray, while I was black and white in big irregular splotches. "I love his little crooked face. I think he is smiling."

"You have to go get him some food, and some litter," she said. "He already knows about using the litter box."

"Tonight?"

"Well yes."

"It's snowing."

"I know it's snowing. I just came in. But there's no store on the way home from the museum, and I didn't want to keep him out any longer."

"I'm not going out in this."

"I think you should. He is probably hungry." She was right about that. I held my breath.

"Oh all right."

"The snow is beautiful," she said. "You'll be glad."

•

She tore up some newspaper in a box, set it on the floor of the bathroom, and put me down in it. Just in time too. I was about to burst and didn't know where to go. I was not prepared to poop but I peed and she was delighted.

While he was out she took a bath. She turned on the water and took off all her clothes and got down on the floor and played with me while the tub was filling up. I can't get used to humans having so much bare skin, with just a few small patches of fur. It's as if they have some horrible disease. It doesn't seem to bother them, though. They like to get naked, I later observed. I can't imagine what it would be like to wear clothes. What is the point? Apparently they get cold. They are always talking about it.

She stood on one foot and lifted the other over the edge into the tub, which was up on little feet. She very slowly stepped in and lowered herself down inside the tub, disappearing behind the high sides. "It's all right," she said, and just sank into the water. Ick!

I sat there happily enough until I realized this was my chance to look around. I discovered a rocking chair in the bedroom and a tall chest of drawers and a silver radiator under the window hissing and clanking softly to itself. The wood floors were slick so I had to go slowly. There were only a few small rugs, with great stretches of bare floor in between. I could barely keep my feet under me. I was glad no one was watching, they would have laughed.

The closet door was closed so I headed

through the other doorway into the narrow kitchen. I would have liked to see what was up on the counters, but I couldn't jump that high. I was still so little I could hardly jump at all. Instead I was stuck in the bottom of a canyon with dust balls and disgusting scraps of old lettuce. The living room was larger. Practically the only furniture besides the harpsichord was a small table with two wooden chairs and a canvas sling chair that didn't look too comfortable. I was tired. I tried curling up on the mattress on the floor in the corner, which was reasonably cozy. I needed to go to sleep immediately but I felt too exposed. I skidded and stumbled over to a small desk and found my way into a dark narrow space behind a bottom drawer and I was out.

•

When I woke up they were coming into the room talking.

"He must be here someplace. He can't have just vanished. Where was he the last time you saw him?"

"He was with me."

"In the tub?"

"No, don't be silly, in the bathroom. He was fine."

I heard the man make little kissing sounds and then call in a high little voice, "Here, kitty. Here, kitty kitty kitty kitty. Here, kitty kitty." It was all I could do not to go right out but for some reason I hesitated. "Does he have a name?"

"Not yet."

"Here, pussy-wussy. Here, catta-watta." Kiss-kiss-kiss.

"He was right here."

"Well where is he now? Did I imagine this whole thing? Was it a dream? Maybe there never was a cat. But there must be some reason I walked six blocks in a blizzard to buy cat food."

"He might be in the closet."

"The closet door was closed." If I was careful I could see them without them seeing me. She was wrapped in a white bathrobe with a towel around her head, dripping a little, leaving wet footprints. He said, "They are both closed. I always close doors. You didn't open them, did you, and shut him in?" He looked in the closet, but of course I wasn't there.

He came straight toward me and leaned down and looked under the desk but I ducked out of sight. I don't know why. Well, I do know. They seemed slightly deranged. I was alarmed.

"He must be hiding," he said. "Why would he hide?"

"You're making him nervous."

"Me? You're the one who thinks he's missing."

"Well he *is* missing," she said. "I think he is inside the wall. He is crawling around inside the walls and can't find his way out. The poor little thing!" They went into the other room.

"How could he get into the walls?"

"He probably crawled into the dumb waiter."

Can that be right? What would a dumb waiter be doing here, and how could I crawl into him. I still have no idea what this means, but that's what they said.

"There is no way he could get into the dumb waiter," the man said. "Look how high the counter is."

"He could jump up there easily."

"Oh I don't think so, he's tiny."

"You know nothing about animals. Cats are amazing."

"I had a dog when I was a boy. I can relate to another sentient being. I had a cat briefly when I was living in the Village but Marco sent it away. I am not insensitive. Give me a little credit."

"I think he has fallen down the dumb waiter.

It probably goes clear down to the basement. You have to go down and look. He may still be alive."

"You think he's dead!?"

"Well he may be. We have to face reality. I'm terribly sorry to put you through all this. I realize it is completely my fault. You know how I am when I am in the water."

"Don't be ridiculous."

"Don't tell me not to be ridiculous."

"I mean, aren't you getting a little carried away?"

"Are you going to go down there or am I?"

"I can't go down there. What am I going to tell Mrs. Johnson?"

I was wondering what had happened to dinner. If they thought I was dead they might not feed me. I probably should have just coolly gone out and walked up to them as best I could and smiled and everything would have been fine, but they were freaking me out. I thought I had better play along so I had another nap.

•

Evidently the woman took matters into her own hands because the next thing I knew an old lady in fluttering veils with wild gray hair sticking out every which way came noisily in from the hall and immediately attacked the man. She did not actually bite and claw him, but her voice was sharp. "I told you. No pets," she said. I wanted to jump her but I thought I might be dreaming.

"I have to talk to you," he said.

"You're damn right you do. What is this woman doing in my house? Why is she waking me up in the middle of the night?"

"It's only nine," the young woman said, coming in behind her.

"I know what time it is. Where is this cat? I want it out of here."

"Mrs. Johnson, please, I beg you," the man said. He looked like he was about to cry. "I am so sorry. I never meant this to happen. You know Miss Wallace, from Denver, I introduced you. This is just a foolish misunderstanding. I should have come down myself. I'm sure it's nothing."

"The people before you had a dog that was nothing but trouble. I won't even tell you. A monster. The people upstairs had a snake that ate my gerbils. The people before them had a monkey. Enough is enough."

"I am so sorry," he said.

"I just want to look," the young woman said.

12

"I don't want him to starve. I don't want him lying there with a broken back suffering."

That sounded like my cue so I walked out where they could see me. Nobody moved. Nobody said anything. I took another wobbly step. The old lady stepped back. The other two looked at each other.

The man squatted down, making his little kissing sounds and holding his hand out. I avoided the hand and went around behind him and brushed against him and let him scoop me up. He held me out to the old lady but she threw up her hands and backed away, hissing. I tried to hiss back at her but it came out a laugh. She turned and went out. The young woman followed her into the hall. "Thank you, Mrs. Johnson, I'm so relieved. Sorry to get you out of bed."

Meanwhile the man had taken me into the kitchen and set me down on the counter while he opened a can of food. Thank heaven! He put it down on the floor. I started to jump down but it was too far. He put me down on the floor and watched me chow down, and it finally dawned on me that he was my person. I had thought she was. Well, whatever. They both seemed a little unbalanced.

The young woman came back, laughing. "Did you see? He was laughing at her," she said.

"It isn't funny," he said. "We may be thrown out in the street, or have to get rid of him."

"I can't take him back."

"We may have to move. I'm not sure I like living way out here in Brooklyn anyway."

"She'll come around. Why should she care if we have a cat? What are you going to call him?"

"Charles."

"That's not really a cat name."

"It is now."

Chapter 2

Their names, I figured out, were David and Doreen. I was right, they were flighty, but they were good-hearted and we got along. I slept on the bed with them so I came to know them pretty well, if a cat can ever really know a person. Doreen was transparent, her moods as different as sun and rain. David was harder to read, busy with affairs in the outside world, often preoccupied. He eventually came to realize that I could understand English, especially *his* well-formed, grammatical English, though I did not always know exactly what he meant or, for that matter, why most people said the particular things they said, which sometimes only stirred up trouble.

One morning at breakfast, for example, David said, "What a beautiful day! What are your plans?"

"You know I don't have any plans."

"You are not trapped here. You don't have to wait for me. You can do things, you're an independent person."

"We could go to the zoo."

"I have to work. Anyway, I can't deal with the

zoo. I feel too sorry for the animals. You can go."

"Are you trying to get rid of me?"

"Why don't you go to the museum? Give Lucy a call."

"She's your friend, she doesn't want to see me."

He went around the table, knelt on the floor beside her chair, took both of her hands in his, and said, "Darling, I have to work. Try to understand. I am trying to write a play. I have to have some time alone. I can't do it while you are talking to me or waiting for me to entertain you. Don't take it personally, please. I don't know what to do. I don't have anyplace else to work."

"You could go to the library."

"I don't want to go to the library."

"I should go back to Denver."

"No, no. I want you to be here. I love you. I only need a couple of hours a day. Go for a walk. Or just stay in the other room. Which room do you prefer? Either one is all right with me."

"I won't talk."

"I really have to be alone."

"Well let me get dressed."

He stood up. "We should hum. We haven't been humming, that's our problem." She nodded,

16

and he led her over to a small rug, where they sat down cross-legged on fat round black cushions facing each other. He put his hand on his lower belly and hummed a deep low note, taking big breaths and humming as long as he could, breathing, humming. She started humming too, humming a version of the same note until their hums melted together. After quite a bit of that, he moved his hand to his heart and hummed a higher note, which she again matched. Then they put their hands on their heads and hummed a high note, sitting up very straight, locked on each other's eyes, madly humming. I felt it vibrate my skull, and I very quietly joined in, pretending not to pay any attention, not wanting to intrude. Then there was silence, and we all felt much more harmonious.

A little later she put on her coat and went out. Before she was even gone he had brought out a typewriter, set it down on the little desk, rolled in a sheet of paper, and started typing, not very fast, a few words, then a pause, muttering to himself, a few more words, sometimes a whole line of words, and so on. When the daylight faded, he turned on the lights and kept typing. He picked me up and put me in his lap and touched me with his fingers when he was thinking. I liked the sharp, light, intermittent tapping sounds, the ding of the bell, the purr and chunk when he pushed the carriage back for another line. He carefully covered three pages with words all the way from the top to the bottom and was stalled halfway down a fourth when Doreen reappeared. He had already dumped me to go look out the window a few times and even opened the door and listened for her footsteps in the hall. When he heard her coming he quickly pulled the page out of the typewriter, put it under the others, and slipped them into a drawer. He was standing up looking slightly guilty when she opened the door.

"There you are."

"What are you doing?"

"I'm fine. I mean, I just finished. I didn't think you would be gone so long."

"Why are you standing there like that?"

"I'm just here, glad you're home. Did you have a good time?"

"Did you do anything about dinner?"

"Was I supposed to?"

"Well somebody has to. It's seven o'clock."

"Are you hungry?"

"No thank you, I ate."

"Really? What about me?"

"You said you wanted me to be independent."

"Not about dinner. I think we should have dinner together every night unless we make some specific other arrangement. Can we agree on that?"

"At what time?"

"Well, at seven, I think, unless we're going to the theatre. Six-thirty at the latest if we're going to the theatre. I can do it, if you like. I'm sorry about tonight, I was working, I forgot all about it."

"I'll do it. Just tell me what you want."

"Don't be like that."

"Like what? I'm agreeing with you. We will have dinner at seven after this. I will make it. You can help."

"I can make a few things."

"I thought you never cooked."

"Well I have been living alone for the past year and a half, and I'm too broke to go out all the time, so I cope, you know? I'd like to be able to cook. You can teach me. Will you?"

"Do you mean it?"

"Yes, I do. I have so much to learn. I know I'm a lot older than you are. But the reality is, there's no difference. You are you just as much as I am me, and vice versa, if you know what I mean."

I was thinking about dinner and gave David a look, standing by the kitchen door and cocking my head, which I know they think is cute. He didn't immediately get it but then I saw him realize, and he got the rest of the can out of the refrigerator. I have my doubts about canned cat food, I know it's full of artificial ingredients and god knows what, but it is irresistibly delicious.

•

One weekend David borrowed his cousin's car and we went to the country. I had only been in a car once before, when I huddled up against my brothers and sisters in a corner of a cardboard box. Being on my own with no place to settle down did something weird to my head. I didn't know what Doreen was doing sitting there staring straight ahead so I didn't want to sit on her lap. Insanely restless, I prowled around looking for some kind of peace that I couldn't find, and heard myself making deep growling sounds that wanted to turn into scorching howls. I managed to stop eventually, but not completely. It made them just as nervous as I felt.

'We need some kind of traveling box for him," David said.

"We should tranquilize him," Doreen said. "Next time I'll give him something."

We eventually stopped in the middle of nowhere, left the car, climbed a hill through the woods—Doreen carried me in her coat—and spent the night in a cabin with rough wood floors, lit by candles and a lantern, warmed by a woodstove. I had never heard quiet before. It was heavenly. I felt completely peaceful in the silence.

In the morning the sun was shining and they opened up one whole side of the house. I found a patch of sunlight and cleaned myself up. David and Doreen were sitting outside talking quietly. Nothing was happening. I went over to the edge of the floor and looked at them and thinking, why not? I jumped down onto the ground, which was soft and uneven, fragrant with crumbled dry leaves, pine needles, moss, lichen, pleasing under paw. I stayed close by, I didn't want to lose my bearings. It didn't look like there was anything to eat out there.

•

They observed a "day of silence" every seventh day. It made me nervous the first couple of times they did it. I thought something was wrong. They reminded each other the night before, and

21

then not a word was spoken the whole next day. Occasionally one of them forgot and a phrase started to slip out, only to be nipped off with an oops and a shrug. It made them noticeably more mellow and relaxed. David took the phone off the hook and put a pillow over it.

David had suggested this, describing some kind of breakthrough moment when he stopped speaking for several days when he was in the country with friends. "Not talking powers up other forgotten levels of communication," he told her. "You can't explain yourself or apologize or make excuses. What you do speaks for itself. I love words but they get in the way of other languages, looks, touch, body moves, little noises, expressions. Kisses are the language of love. We think words can do everything but they're no substitute really. We can still misunderstand each other but we can't make it worse by trying to analyze our feelings. Gurdjieff says emotion is a separate brain. It is an error to be logical about it."

Doreen was dubious at first, but she tried it and found she liked it. "We're more even when you can't talk me into a corner," she said the next day.

"You can't fend me off by playing dumb,"

"We're both playing dumb."

"Oh, right. Ha ha."

It was relaxing for me too and I looked forward to it every week. It made them more like regular animals. I didn't have to figure out what they were talking about, which was always confusing. I never knew whether to believe them or not: they were often deluded. I was fascinated by how transparently they maneuvered for advantage and struggled to justify themselves and figure out what to do next according to what they thought the other one thought, meanwhile clinging to what they thought they thought themselves. They were always searching for some intangible satisfaction, some other situation than the one they were in. It was odd.

•

"Can we have a party?" she said. She wanted to meet his friends and it was almost Christmas. He thought it was a good idea. They spent a whole day making invitations and handmade envelopes to mail them in. Other people he called on the phone.

"Will you invite Marco?" she wanted to know.

"I don't think he would come."

"I want to meet him."

"Why?"

"Because he is important to you. I think you are still in love with him."

"I probably am," he said. "I don't stop loving people I once loved. I love them forever."

"Do you love him more than me?"

"It is completely different. I love you for being you and I loved him for being him. The dynamic is not the same. Anyway it's over. It's been almost two years. He has a new boyfriend, and I have you."

"Don't you want to see him?"

"I do, but maybe not at a party. He would feel manipulated."

"Go ahead and invite him. Sincerity is better than considering. Why would you not?"

"I don't want to be rejected. In my dreams he always runs away from me just when we start to get close. All right. We will send him an invitation."

Having decided to have an afternoon party and serve cider and cookies, they pored over cookbooks together, and Doreen spent two days making cookies in a dozen whimsical varieties. They decorated the living room festively with pine boughs and ribbons.

•

I wasn't sure what I should do on the day of the party. I was intensely curious, of course. The first time the doorbell rang I ran out into the hall with them and looked down the stairwell. Several people came clumping up, led by a large man in a black cape and wide-brimmed hat with a green parrot on his beringed hand that turned out on closer inspection to be stuffed. Right behind him were a tall black woman with tangled gray locks, two blond men, one tall and balding, the other small and cute, a bearded man carrying an oddly shaped case, and a regular middle-aged couple, the man bearing a bottle of wine. I rapidly retreated into the bedroom and missed whatever anyone said; the living room was a babble of voices and I couldn't make sense of anything. I hid under the bed, cowering, trembling in spite of myself; I wanted to be sociable but I couldn't do it. More people came in and threw coats on the bed. I calmed down and when nobody was there I emerged and burrowed in among the coats, trying to be invisible. People were enjoying themselves. It was nice to be there.

I could see through into the living room, where everyone quieted down for a little concert by David on harpsichord with his bearded friend playing a violin. Ah, that explained the case. Normally I liked to sit with David while he played, but I didn't want to attract attention so I stayed put. The music was sublime; I would have liked them to play all afternoon. When they stopped there was a little applause and cooing, and the babble gradually rose again.

David came into the bedroom leading by the hand a rumpled fellow with red lips and curly hair. "I'm glad you are here, Max" he said, "I need to talk to you." If I didn't move they wouldn't see me.

"What is it, darling?"

"Listen, are you going to be in my play or not?"

"Are you asking me?"

"What?! Didn't you get my message? I thought you were avoiding me."

"No. I only got an invitation to the party, which I thought was very sweet, she is very sweet, my dear, very. I think you're mad. I knew you were doing this play and I was hoping to hear from you, frankly, but I didn't, and that was that. I assume you have someone else. Some pig. I hate you. Don't you have anything to drink?"

"There isn't anyone else. No one else can play

the king. I wrote it for you."

"What king are we talking about?"

"Wilhelm Friedrich. I have some Jack Daniels."

"That would certainly help," he said, with a mean look in my direction.

David fetched the bottle and a small glass and poured him a drink. "Can you do it? Will you do it?"

"Get yourself a glass. We will drink to it. I am at your service, master. Tell me what to do."

"Oh thank heavens! That's what I needed to hear. We will start rehearsals immediately after New Year's. I will give you a script and a copy of the schedule. Four weeks rehearsal, and then we open for two or three weeks depending on whether people come. How are you?"

"I'm still walking." He sat down on the bed heavily and reached for me. I pulled back, hissing and baring my little claws. He put down his drink, hissed and made claws right back at me, and grabbed me.

"This is Charles," David said. "Charles, this is Max."

"I hate cats," Max said and threw me on the floor. I went back under the bed.

"I heard you're not, pardon the expression,

27

doing speed anymore."

"Wasn't it fun! Ah yes! The good old days!"

"It was fun until it wasn't," David said. "I couldn't believe your, what, stamina."

"Is Marco coming? I haven't seen him in months. He never answers his doorbell."

"I hear he's out of town on a gig."

"I can't wait for rehearsals to start. Here's to our renewed collaboration." I heard a dull clink.

"I'm psyched," David said. "You will love this role. You'll be great!"

•

After everybody left, when it was just David and Doreen, I crept back into the living room. They were gathering abandoned glasses and plates and emptying ashtrays. Doreen picked me up and kissed me, saying, "There you are, are you all right? Did you have a good time?"

David went into the kitchen and started washing dishes. I kneaded her shoulder to let her know I was happy but she didn't seem to like it and dumped me. She stood in the kitchen doorway watching him.

"You have such interesting friends," she said,

"What? Oh yes, I do, I'm glad you like them."

"I didn't say that."

"Well, some of them. I know some of them are a little hard to take."

"They must think I am very dumb."

He turned off the water. "They don't know anything about you. It takes time in a new place," he said, drying his hands. "I can do this later. Let's go to bed."

"Your friend Max was condescending."

"Oh he's that way with everyone. You can't take him seriously. Today he was unusually calm. What did he say?"

"He said my paintings were sweet."

"They are sweet. You're sweet. Sweet is good. Sweet is what we need more of. I couldn't go on being mean and desperate and bitter. It was ruining my health and morale."

"I am not a piece of candy."

"Of course not, but you are my favorite cookie." He took her hand and started nibbling on her fingers, smacking his lips.

"I am a real artist," she said.

"I know you are."

"Don't humor me."

"I'm just trying to have fun," he said. "Don't be so serious."

"It's not a joke. They don't take me seriously at all. They think you're just pretending."

"Sweetie, please! Lighten up. You're wonderful. We had a wonderful party. I am so happy with you. I love you. I love our life. Everything is better. Your cookies were a triumph." He managed to get his arms around her and she gave in and let him embrace her.

"Did people like them?"

"They loved them."

"You're right. I am such an egomaniac."

"No you're not, you're fine. I love you. Do you like it here? Are you happy? Are you going to be all right?"

"I will be if you love me."

"Why don't we get in bed? Wouldn't that be nice?"

"It's only seven-thirty."

"That's all right, we can get up again. There aren't any rules."

So they went to bed and made love and everything was all right. When they quieted down they were close and relaxed and nothing could ever take that feeling away.

They got up again later and finished cleaning up. Sipping bourbon, David made an omelet and a simple green salad for their supper.

Chapter 3

The love thing is important to them, I can see. They do a lot of nuzzling and rubbing against each other, I can understand that. In the bed they don't always lie still but also squirm and thrash around under the covers and sometimes get quite carried away, sometimes for quite a while. I never know when they're going to start. They are perfectly calm, I think they're going to sleep, and then he starts licking her ear or something, and pretty soon they are fairly wild, throwing the covers off, with no regard for my comfort, pressing themselves together, making squishy sounds and panting and moaning. I get up and leave as soon as they start. It makes them happy, obviously. Sometimes they do it in the morning. Or they start hugging and kissing in the middle of the afternoon and take off all their clothes and do it. I don't mind. I have found several cozy spots in the living room, and there's a hot water pipe behind the tub I like to get close to. Then I come back after the storm has passed.

They had several rehearsals for David's play in the living room, but I stayed away, not wanting to tangle with Max. I emerged whenever David practiced the music, playing along with a nice guy with a ponytail and a guitar, who taught him how to improvise on the harpsichord. Doreen joined in on an odd-looking Indian instrument that made a continuous hum, mmmzzzmmmzzz. Then they started going elsewhere to rehearse and were out every evening for weeks. I gathered that the play was not an entirely happy experience. The first stage manager quit in a huff, and the actors had a hard time getting along.

"You know Max was drunk tonight, don't you?" Doreen asked as they were getting ready for bed.

"I know, I know. He was swigging bourbon in the dressing room. So was Fred."

"Fred was inspired tonight."

"It's too much," David said. "He is too precious. The two of them are horribly mean to Petey and Maude, who are so good and working so hard. I talked to Max afterwards. Fred ran right out. He is doing two other shows and doesn't have time for me. Max was better off on amphetamine but I guess it couldn't go on."

"Are you horribly disappointed?"

"No, no! It's the most beautiful thing I've ever done. I love it! I wish Max would get it together though. He was sublime in rehearsal but he has never dared to go there in performance. I guess it was too real and it scared him. No, I love it, and I love playing in the little band with you, my darling."

"I feel like I'm fading into the wallpaper," she said.

"That's what the music is," he said, "like the candles and the black and gold backcloth. I'm sure it's tiring. I don't know how you can do it. You are a hero of art."

•

The play ended, and everything went back to what I took to be normal. I thought, ah, this is what the real world is like, this is my life, and I was just beginning to get my head around it being that way forever when instead of continuing with what they were doing, my people changed the rules in some way, and we embarked on the long sequence of unpredictable and confusing developments that made me the cat I became.

David went away for a few days. Doreen cried, talked to her sisters on the telephone, packed her suitcase, unpacked, and spent a whole day painting pictures of me. The evening after he came back, after their dinner, he drew her to him, had her sit on his lap, kissed her and nibbled her ear, and said, "Don't you think we should get married?"

"Is it time to talk about that?"

"Well, you want to have a baby, don't you? I know *I* want to have a baby, but you're the one who has to do it."

"Yes, I want to have your baby. But we don't have to get married," she said.

"I know, I am not a great fan of marriage either, but it probably would be easier just to do it so the baby will have an official father. I mean, you and I would know, but other people, I don't know. It would certainly make your father feel better. What do you think?"

"You're probably right."

"I had a realization on the plane looking down on Brooklyn as I was flying out. I couldn't see the house but I could imagine you down here all by yourself. What would happen to you if my plane crashed? I felt like I wasn't taking care of you. What would you do?"

"I don't know."

"That's what I mean. If we were married you would at least have a place to live. I know that doesn't sound very romantic. The point is, I

floor and a piano. Down a slippery flight of stairs was a theatre, not very big, rows of seats on steps facing an open floor with many lights on the ceiling. There was also an office, dressing rooms, a lobby, the works. Other people came and went down there, but we were alone upstairs. The afternoon sun was shining in and David and Doreen took off their clothes and did the love thing on the living room floor, which seemed to have particular significance.

They had rehearsals in the theatre, going down every night after dinner, shutting me in upstairs, and after a few weeks I started to feel at home.

"I'm going to take Charles to the dress rehearsal," David said one afternoon. "I don't have to do anything but watch. It is out of my control at this point. The actors will do whatever they do. He can sit on my lap."

That evening they went down without me as usual, and I thought he had forgotten, but after a while he reappeared. I was waiting by the door. He started to lean down but then said, "Just a minute," closed the door, went to the other end of the room, and had a little smoke. I liked the smell of his smoke. A few puffs now and then obviously gave him pleasure.

When he opened the door I went out on the landing and he thoughtfully carried me down the unpleasantly slippery stairs and into the theatre, where a dense forest had been built on the stage, many fake tree trunks going up to the ceiling, leaves hanging down. The floor sloped this way and that, covered with grass, a bush, a big fallen log, all fake. The lights changed and people of all ages came in and talked and moved around, sometimes dancing, sometimes rolling around on the floor. There were people up in the trees too, you could see their legs, playing music and twittering like birds. Doreen was disguised as an old lady and acted very funny. It got almost dark and everybody went to sleep and the log and the bush changed places. It was quite amazing.

The next day the people who really lived there came home, Sam and Millie, an older couple. All four of them were old friends and obviously fond of each other, but Millie didn't like me.

"I didn't know you had a cat," she said, sniffing suspiciously. "You didn't say anything about a cat."

"He's very nice," Doreen said.

"I'm sorry," David said, "I thought it would be

all right."

"You should have asked."

"You might have said no. And then what would we have done?"

"We couldn't leave him there," Doreen said.

"Well anyway, we're out of here," David said, "and no harm done. Thank you so much for letting us stay. We had a wonderful time. How was your trip?"

"It was good."

"We stopped in Taos on the way back from California. It's so beautiful there, it's magical."

"I love it," David said. "I go there every chance I get."

"Thank you for looking after the theatre," said Sam. "I can't wait to see your play."

"We'll be back in a couple of hours."

So we moved again, to a house with three rooms, a little like our apartment, but with practically no furniture. The bed was full of water and moved when you sat on it. David thought it was sexy but it made Doreen queasy so they didn't have as much fun as he'd hoped.

Chapter 4

The next few months were a nightmare, one move after another, with no rhyme or reason to them. First there was their "honeymoon." They picked me up right after the "wedding" and off we went. Doreen's mother had given them her "Mustang," and they had a new box for me, which was bigger, made out of plywood with a door on one end and an arched top made of wire mesh. Doreen put several layers of newspaper on the floor. David popped me in and shut the door, saying, "Sorry," but I'm not sure he was sorry. I didn't like it but what could I do? I howled the whole time that first evening in the car. The next morning and every road day after that Doreen forced one of the weird pills down my throat so much of it was a blur.

For some days we lived in a log cabin with Navajo rugs and a fireplace, and I started to relax. I wasn't supposed to be there so sometimes they put me in the box but mostly it was all right. David wore cowboy boots and went horseback riding every day. Doreen went a few times but she said it made her feel sick.

"It's so wonderful," he said, "I wish you

would come. There are beautiful places up in the mountains, meadows covered with wildflowers up to the horse's belly."

"I want to but the motion is too much for me."

"Are you ill?"

"No, it's perfectly normal in the first trimester. I'll be fine in a few weeks."

"I hate to go off and leave you. I mean, it's our honeymoon."

"No, no, you go, have a good time. I'm perfectly happy. Charles will keep me company. I have a whole stack of books."

He was gone all day. She put me in the box in the closet when the maid came in to make the bed. She made a fire and read for a while and then painted a picture of me curled up in an armchair. She showed it to me but as usual I didn't get it, it just looked like swirls on a piece of paper. Later she took me out for a walk. The ground was dusty and prickly. We went down to a stream rushing wildly through rocks, foaming and flashing in the sunlight. We sat on a boulder and gazed at the water for a long time. We were looking for fish but we didn't see any.

Then the three of us got back in the car and traveled for a while, stopping in a different motel every night, until we arrived in "Santa Barbara," which had a whole different set of smells. We lived in a house with shag carpet and a large cage full of finches, which were fascinating to me. I was getting big and strong by now, and Doreen was afraid I would get into the birdcage, which I would have done if I could find a way in, but it was pretty well constructed, and she was careful about keeping the door latched. I couldn't figure out what the birds were up to. They were stupid little things, fluttering from branch to branch. shifting their feet and fluffing their feathers, looking at me with empty eyes. Some of them were being picked on for some reason, other birds pecking all the feathers out around their necks, which left them looking sick and pitiful. Those birds were vicious. I wanted to kill them, and eat them.

I was glad when we moved again, into a set of bare little rooms with painted floors, which David and Doreen gradually furnished from the "thrift shop," which made me think we were going to stay. They let me go outside. That was exciting: I was ready for adventure. It was pretty much bare dirt out there, the top of a hill, olive trees and tall eucalyptus trees rustling in the ocean breeze, with the remains of a garden, box beds with nothing in them but a few dead weeds. No one lived in the big house.

It was nice to see them so happy together, which made a kind of glow that rubbed off on me. I was happy too.

She had given him a guitar for a wedding present. He had a scrap of paper with notes on it and taught himself to play enough chords to sing a few songs. David's mother and father came over for dinner and he sang them "Down by the O-hi-o," which made his parents look at each other strangely.

Doreen got a job. She went off every day and came back exhausted and smelling of leather. David did some typing while she was gone, but they were worried about "money."

"You're going to be too pregnant to work, and then what will we do?" he said. "I need to get a job."

"What are you going to do?"

"I'd like to be a butler," he said. "I am very good at polishing silver. I like nice things. You're a good cook. We could be a 'couple.' There are a lot of rich people around here who need good servants."

"Are you serious?"

"Why not? You think it would be beneath us?"

"You're an intellectual."

"Not really."

"You're an educated person."

"What does that mean? That I can't do things? I can't work? I have to just think and read and write, words words words? I am sick of it. I put in an application at the newspaper but I don't want to work for the newspaper."

"You could be a mailman."

"I'd like that. How are you doing? You never say anything about work."

"There isn't much to say. Everybody else speaks Spanish. We sit at long tables and tap tap all day making our little patterns. We make some nice stuff. You wouldn't like it. You'd be bored."

"I'm sure you're right."

"You don't want a job."

"I do. I am tired of having to motivate myself. Making myself start takes so much effort that I don't have enough left to actually accomplish anything."

"Are you writing a play?"

"What's the sense? I can't do another play. I have to do something I get paid for."

"Well what do you want to do? What have you done that you really liked doing?"

"Apart from directing plays?"

"Yes."

"Well, making my harpsichord. That was wonderful. I loved it. I loved puttering away at it all day with the light changing and actually getting somewhere, all those bits of wood and wire gradually turning into an instrument that I could play music on, the most fantastic intricate passionate music. I could do that."

"Could you?"

"I'll write to Wolfgang. He sold his harpsichord kit business, but he can tell me what the possibilities are."

"I think you should."

"I will."

"I can't go on working too much longer. It's already getting hard to reach the table, and I'm not sure the banging is good for the baby."

"I know."

"You have to take care of me."

"I want to. Oh darling, you're so precious."

•

I sensed that there were other animals out there, not necessarily friendly, so I didn't venture too far from our little cottage on the hill. I took the precaution of marking a periphery so they would know the house was mine and stay back, and I marked a few places inside while I was at it.

Something was bothering my people, something to do with me. I heard Doreen say, "We have to get Charles fixed. He is not a kitten anymore."

"I hate to do it," David said.

"He'll be better off."

"He won't be able to have sex. I wouldn't want to not have sex."

"It's not the same."

"How do you know?"

Whatever they were talking about, they were not asking me.

She changed the subject. "Do you hear buzzing? Listen." They were standing in the middle of the bedroom.

"I hear it," he said. "Where is it coming from?"

She put her ear against the wall next to the window. "It's here, listen."

He put his ear to the wall. "What is it?"

"Bees. There is a bee colony inside the wall."

"Good heavens."

I had heard this right away, I don't know why

they were so surprised.

She looked out the window at an angle. "Look, there they go, see them all coming and going?" He joined her. It was not that interesting, but it seemed to excite them. I knew what was next. I left them there watching the bees.

I tried to hold myself back, knowing it was probably unwise to go too far or stay out late, but I had a kind of craving for something, something drew me, something more than curiosity, and I gradually gave in. I didn't know what I was looking for. I stalked as if I was stalking something. I pounced as if I was pouncing on something. I prowled farther than I had ever prowled before. I went down the hill and came to the back fence of another house. There was another cat there, the one I was after. I went in. She had her back up, tail stiff, fur standing up on her neck. She was beautiful. She hissed, I hissed, and then we came together with a lot of squalling. I suppose that's the love thing, though people are a lot quieter about it, and spend more time. A woman came running out of the house with a broom screaming, "Scat, cat!" but by then it was over anyway.

All of a sudden it was dark. I could see well

enough out in the open but not back in the shadows. Something was in the bushes but I didn't know what. It was going along with me, making a lot of noise. I stopped and it stopped too. I thought it might be creeping closer. I ran and heard it running too. I wasn't quite sure where I was. I came up against a wall I didn't remember seeing before, and found myself blocked in a corner. I panicked, and right then this horrible smelly dark gray thing came charging at me and knocked me down and bit me in the shoulder. It got on top of me, heavy, snarling and slobbering. I thought it was going to kill me. I twisted and clawed as hard as I could. It didn't seem too swift. I think I caught it in the eye. It suddenly pulled back with a shiver and turned and lumbered away. I never did have a good look at it.

I was hurt. I was afraid it would come back. I stayed there for a long time, under some boards. I couldn't even lick my wound, I was so tired. The night went dead quiet. I eventually realized I was not going to die, crept out, keeping low, and made my way back to the house, which was dark. I was touched that my people had left the porch light on for me, not that I needed it. I feebly scratched at the door but nobody came.

Doreen found me in the morning, and they took me to the doctor, who gave me a shot and sewed up my shoulder. She did something at my rear end too. None of it hurt, until later, and then not for long. They took me back home and were very nice to me, and pretty soon I forgot all about it, except in my dreams.

Chapter 5

Doreen was about to be taken over by having a baby and David had to get a job, there was no way around it. The job he found, as a result of letters and phone calls to his harpsichord-maker friend, was at the opposite end the country, in "Connecticut," and would entail another drastic displacement.

Wherever I am I want to stay there, but this time I was ready to move. Santa Barbara was too dry, the leaves dusty after months of no rain, our abandoned hilltop hideaway parched and creepy. I lay in the sun on the stoop and felt myself getting fat and lazy, but there was nothing I wanted to do, no place I wanted to go.

This must have been an epic drive, but most of the time I was zonked in my box on the back seat, only fragmentarily aware of where we were or what they were saying. On the Navajo reservation David saw a cloud shaped like a thunderbird and they took it for a glorious omen. In Denver they traded up to a larger trailer. In "Missouri" they visited Doreen's parents and brothers, who were excited about her bulging belly. We stopped in "Ithaca" for David's sister's wedding, which entailed a crowded party at a farmhouse. I hate parties but I sometimes get turned on by them in spite of myself. I followed David down into the basement with another man and looked around while they smoked beside the furnace. There were mice! I didn't see them right away, but I knew they were there. As I hoped, the humans forgot about me and left me down there all night, and I'm afraid I overindulged. But that's what parties are about, right?

David's father rode with us the rest of the way to "Stonington." His long stiff frame barely fit in beside my box in the back seat. It was too uncomfortable for him so David put the box in the trailer and let me lie on a towel on the seat. "He is tranquilized, he is not going anywhere anyway," David said. I don't know that "tranquilized" is quite the word for the demented fog I was in. I mindlessly clawed the back of David's father's hand when he was probably just trying to be friendly, and it bled extensively. I felt terrible. David was mad at me, but his father was nice about it. I didn't want to be drugged. I didn't want to go on long car trips. None of it was my fault.

We finally made it to our destination and checked into a little inn where we had a tiny room.

The bathroom was shared so the only place to put my litter box was under the bed. I didn't like it any more than they did. It was horribly embarrassing when I had to poop, and they made a gigantic scene about the stink, which woke them up in the middle of the night. They both leapt out of bed, gasping and groaning in hushed voices. David threw the French doors open wide, waving his arms around wildly, while Doreen took the box off to the toilet, thank you very much. I slipped out onto the narrow iron balcony and discovered that we were in a beautiful spot, looking out on a cove full of bobbing boats, with a pretty little formal yard down below, the moon shining brightly.

"What a stinko!" Doreen said as they got back under the covers. "Leave the doors open. I can't believe it!"

"This bed is impossible," David said, making it squeak as he squirmed. "I keep falling into the middle."

"I can't help it," she said.

"I'm not blaming you."

"I feel like I'm sleeping with a bowling ball," she said. There was another fit of squeaking and rustling.

"Can I still fuck you?"

"Yes, but you can't lie on top of me."

"I wouldn't think of it. Oh, you're so round and sexy. There's something about it. You really turn me on."

"Come on in. The baby likes it."

And so on. I tuned out, gazing at the moonlit sea.

•

We moved into an upstairs apartment between a busy street and the railroad tracks, and I didn't get out anymore. I didn't care. David went off to work every day and came back smelling of sawdust and turpentine. To pay for the baby, he bought a harpsichord kit from his new boss, Bruno, and built a harpsichord for a friend of his in the living room after work and weekends, listening to a classical radio station in Boston. By the time he was ready for Doreen to paint flowers on the soundboard, she was so big she could barely reach.

They were thrilled at the prospect of having a baby, which bathed the new setting and routine of ordinary life in a glow of contentment that I basked in too. It was harder and harder for Doreen to get comfortable. She spent more and more time in the bathtub. David was enjoying being a simple workman for the moment but not sure what he had got himself into.

"I am working for a madman," he said one night sitting on the floor of the bathroom, Doreen semi-submerged in hot water surrounded by half a dozen candles. "You should hear him on the telephone with the factory in Philadelphia, screaming at them, bellowing, pacing around the office tangling up the phone cord. Bruno is a big man and when he gets worked up he's like a berserk lion."

"What is he so upset about?"

"Some little part that's missing from the boxes that have gone to Germany. Some other part that is an eighth of an inch too thick. I don't know. Anything. It's every day. The prototype is late, or the customs papers are lost. It's always something. He is a fanatic. He had me paint an instrument a hideous color, chartreuse, three careful coats, it took a week, and now he is having me sand it off, by hand. It's insane."

"You should quit."

"It's to teach me a lesson. He is some kind of genius. He was showing me about the special wire he uses, making me listen to one note, over and over, trying to hear how it settles into the pitch and blooms and fades, how a different kind of wire has a different kind of buzz. He is teaching me how to tune, which I've never been good at. He's very smart. He treats me like a complete idiot, and I feel like an idiot. I don't know anything. I have to learn it all from the beginning. I have to learn how to work. So far in my life I've just been sliding along, without traction, without commitment."

"That's not true. You're a wonderful writer."

"Well, that's the way it feels. It changes everything to be a husband and father."

"Are you happy?"

"I've never been so happy in my life. Are you?"

"I am beyond happy. I am the servant of the process. I hardly even exist," she said, flopping around and splashing water over the edge. I jumped out of the way. "Help me get up." He tenderly hoisted her out and dried her off and helped her into the bedroom and after a while we all went to sleep.

•

They drove off somewhere, after a flurry of urgencies and confusion, for the birthing. Left alone in the apartment I strolled through the nondescript rooms with their inadequate rugs as if they were mine, as if I was the sovereign of my destiny, knowing of course that I am not, of course not, and yet content. I am not a wild cat. My worst nightmare is to find myself feral, abandoned. David and Doreen's benevolence is a bit whimsical but they are not irresponsible. I count myself lucky. I can't make much sense of the constant uprootings and repottings they put us through, though. Anyplace is fine. What's the difference?

It was snowing when they came back with the baby, and it went on snowing for a couple of days, which made everything extra quiet and still, the reflection off the snow onto the ceilings setting the rooms afloat in light. They set up a crib next to their bed but the baby was usually under the covers with them, or nursing. Doreen was worried about me jumping into the crib with the baby and hurting it. Not a chance. I did jump in, but it was not pleasant and I jumped right out; I wouldn't have done it again even if she hadn't rigged netting over it. I went upstairs in the daytime, where there were two more rooms, unused. I had nothing against the baby, which was completely helpless. I preferred sleeping at the foot of the bed. I didn't like them breathing on me.

Doreen's mother came for a visit, and I think she started to like me. The mood was cozy and rosy, the little family playing out a story of perfect self-completeness (complete with yours truly). Doreen was still attached to the baby; nursing could put her into an erotic trance. She let David suckle a little too (not something grown cats would do), which gave him some kind of special thrill.

He still had to finish the harpsichord, which kept him busy for several more weeks, painting the outside, putting strings on it, eventually making it play, and then playing it, simple pieces, then more fancy ones, tricky and splashy. I liked the ones that hummed along evenly like machinery. David beamed when his fingers behaved and the music expanded to flood the room. His friend came and liked it and took it away. I was sorry to see it go.

"You should make one for yourself," Doreen said.

"I want to, but I'll have to pay for the parts," he said. "We can't afford it. Anyway I need a break.

I don't want to work on harpsichords all the time, I want to write."

"I don't have anything to do," she said.

"What do you want to do?"

"I never see anyone but you, and you're gone all day."

"I have to work."

"At least you see other people."

"I suppose."

"Well, you do."

"It takes a year in a new place. I could invite Kathy for dinner with her husband the dentist, would you like that? I didn't think we needed anyone else."

"Do you think I'm going crazy?"

"Of course not. It's hormones. Your whole body has to reorganize."

"It's not my body, it's my mind. I feel like I've been erased or painted over."

"Would you like to take an etching class at the community center?"

"Are you serious?"

"I saw something about it on the bulletin board at the market. It's on Monday nights, I think. I'll get you the details."

"I can't leave Joey."

"He can stay with me. I'd like it."

"I can pump some milk for him. Do you think you can handle it?"

"I'm sure I can."

"Oh, that would save my life."

"You need to do something. I understand. Kathy and Jim can come for dinner on Friday, I hope that's all right. I can make spaghetti and a salad if you like."

"No, I'll cook, oh, what'll I make, something special. I want to. I feel better already."

•

That first apartment was a winter rental so we moved again in May to the whole upstairs of a creaky old house high on the hill in town, with a view out over the harbor from their bedroom window. They ripped up the linoleum in the kitchen and scullery, Doreen scraped off the black gunk, and David sanded the maple floor with a big roaring machine and then did the fir in the other rooms. They painted every room a different color, the kitchen red, the living room green, their bedroom lavender, baby Joe's room blue, Doreen's studio white.

David's parents came to visit just as we were moving in, renting a vacation house some miles away. David came home from work wanting to paint another room and complained that instead they had to go visit his parents, but I think he liked it too. I was not invited—sometimes I wished I was a dog—just kidding!

I got the picture when they came home. "Did you see my father teaching him to crawl? He got down on the rug in the living room with him, demonstrating, and Joey started to do it. His arms are not strong enough to hold him up so he kept falling on his face but he got the idea. It was adorable. I haven't seen my father so happy in a long time."

"When are you going to paint my studio?"

"Not tonight. I'm going to bed. I'm exhausted."

"I worked for hours today preparing the surface."

"I can start in the morning. I promised them we would come for lunch. My brother is coming from the city, and my sister is driving down from Vermont. I want them to meet Joey. You too."

She said, "I love your father, but your mother makes me nervous."

"She loves you. She can't help being critical. You have your own ways of doing things. It broke her heart when we moved away, I knew it at the time, but she can't help seeing that you make me happy. It's only for a week. Everything will get done. I hate it as much as you do."

"No, you don't."

"No, of course I don't. I want to give myself to them while they are here. They'll go away and we won't see them for six months or a year. We can afford to be generous."

"You're a good man."

"I try. Be brave, darling. We have all the time in the world."

"I have to start painting another harpsichord soundboard. I promised. Bruno is sending it over on Monday."

"I'll do it. I'll stay up all night. Just not tonight. Have mercy."

"I can do it myself."

"No, I will. We'll do it together tomorrow night, no matter what time we get home. Deal? It will only take a couple of hours."

"That's what you always say."

"Four hours?"

"Four or five."

"I can do that. Now come to bed. You're all tense. Let me rub it out."

And much later: "That's better."

·

The seasons went around. David went to work, and then he got a "grant" to write another play. He rented a room downstairs where I kept him company late at night while he struggled with an electric typewriter, slowly piling up pages. In the daytime Doreen painted watercolors and decorated a succession of harpsichords, including one David made for himself. It was pink! Girlfriends came over for tea, and couples for dinner. Joey started walking and beginning to talk.

One funny thing happened that I didn't entirely witness but managed to piece together from fragments of conversation overheard. I still didn't completely understand what was going on, but I later saw it as a harbinger of what was to come so it is worth telling.

It started when Marco, the person who had not showed up at the Christmas cookie party—how long ago was that?—came for a visit. David had been visiting him whenever he went into the city to deliver a harpsichord. I gleaned that David had lived with Marco in the past and done the love thing with him, he was his "great love," but they no longer did it, they were just friends.

However he still had special feelings for him and wanted him to be Joey's godfather. Doreen was not "jealous," she was fascinated.

David went to pick him up at the train. Just before they came back Doreen's tea-party friend Alicia arrived with two young daughters and husband and an enormous bunch of daffodils. Coming up right behind them into this chaos Marco, small and dark, politely shook everyone's hand but hardly spoke a word, keeping himself contained and carefully looking around, rather cat-like, I thought.

Scooping up Joey, they all tromped down the stairs and went out, and in the confusion I went with them. I never went out in that town so it was exciting. I followed them down a little hill and out across a big open space to the fishing boat pier, which I had looked at out the window many times. It smelled wildly of fish, some good, some not so good. We went out to the end of the pier, which was really a jetty, built out on big rocks. David, who had been carrying Joey, put him into Marco's arms, and Marco climbed down over the rocks to the water, variously followed and observed, where he squatted down, scooped a handful of water out of the harbor, and splashed and patted it on Joey's head. David and Doreen were humming together. Joey squirmed, and Marco laughed, and Alicia flung the bouquet of flowers out onto the softly heaving water.

After dinner David took Marco out for a walk while Doreen put Joey to bed. They came back smelling smoky and before long everybody went to bed. Doreen was not sleepy, however, and David was easily stirred up. They were thinking of doing love, and I was thinking of slipping away when I heard her say in an odd voice, "David."

"Mmm."

"David."

"What is it, darling? Don't you want to?"

"No, I'm fine. I was just thinking…"

"What?"

"Maybe Marco would like to join us."

"Uh, I don't think so."

"Wouldn't you like it?"

"Well…"

"Go ask him. Invite him."

"I can't."

"You know you want to. Go on."

"Just do it with me, just you and me," he said.

"Don't be a wuss. Come on, go get him, I want to. I insist."

"All right. All right." He got out of bed. He was naked and his penis was sticking out. I followed him to the guest room in the opposite corner of the house, pretending of course that I just happened to be going in that direction.

He knocked on the door.

"Come in." I slipped in when David opened the door. Marco was sitting up in bed and looked up from his book as David stepped into the light.

Slightly distracted by me, David said, "Doreen and I would like to invite you to join us in our bed." He looked down at himself and smiled up at Marco.

Marco said, "No, thank you. Thank you very much, but I think not."

"Just thought I'd ask. It was her idea."

"Good night."

"Good night, my dear," said David, and closed the door and went back to Doreen, I imagine. Marco let me sleep on the foot of his bed, and their door was closed when he let me out in the morning.

•

That was not the end of it. A few days later Doreen announced, "I'm going into the city to see Marco. Can I leave Joey with you?"

"What?"

"I called him. I'm going on Saturday, on the train. I'll be back Sunday afternoon. Can I leave Joey with you?"

"I'm fine with Joey, but why are you doing this?"

"I want to."

"Are you planning to seduce him?"

"Yes."

"What? I'm the one who's supposed to have feelings for him, and I don't. I mean, I do, but it's over, I don't want to stir it up again."

"We can all love each other."

"Of course. We do. We all do. But let's keep it simple, can't we?"

"I'm going. You don't really mind, do you?"

"Why should I mind? I love you both. I want you to be happy. It's a little titillating, even. But I don't think it's a good idea. I would advise you to reconsider."

She went anyway, in a dress that clung to her curves. It was rather pleasant to be at home without her, frankly, just the three of us males in the house, a kind of natural sympathy among us that didn't always need to be challenged. David got into the bathtub with Joey and they played for a long time, running the water now and then to warm it up again. David put Joey down in his high-sided bed, but Joey was not happy and couldn't go to sleep. David tried to write but Joey was crying and calling to him. It was not possible to ignore him, and eventually he took him into the big bed and read to him and he was happy and we all slept together.

Doreen was sheepish when she got home the next day. David wanted to know what had happened but she wouldn't talk about it. She was extra affectionate, and they lay down for a late afternoon nap with their door closed for a while. She still hadn't told him anything, but after Joey was in bed it came out that Marco had been very nice, and taken her out to dinner, and they went back to his apartment afterwards, and sat around, very friendly, listening to music, and then when it got late he excused himself and went out and didn't come back. She had been a little scared but mostly humiliated.

Eventually she had gone to sleep. Marco reappeared in the morning just in time to take her in a taxi to the station and see her to her train.

"Oh David, I'm so embarrassed."

"It's all right. You're perfectly all right. It

wasn't real, you know."

"He thinks I'm a fool."

"No, he likes you. He just doesn't want emotional complications. Everything he did was perfectly correct. He is an enlightened being, look at it that way. You can learn a spiritual lesson from it."

"Can you forgive me?"

"I love you. You're funny and sweet. There is nothing to forgive."

"Thank you, thank you, you're so good."

"Remember that. It's not true but it's useful, it's an intention."

"What are you talking about?"

"The next time you're mad at me, or want somebody else. It does hurt a little, hard as I try not to let it."

•

After that I thought everything was fine so imagine my surprise when they started talking about moving again.

"You have to get out from under Bruno, he is beating you down," she said. "Every day he insults and belittles you. How can you stand it?"

"It's just the way he is."

"You have to stand up for yourself."

"I've tried that, but it makes things worse. Today he picked on me about some stupid thing that I had screwed up. It was my own fault, I admitted it and apologized, but he wouldn't stop. He worked himself up till he was bellowing at me in front of the whole shop. I was embarrassed for him."

"What about you? You pretend it doesn't bother you, but it does. I see you slumping, glum. You should quit. You can find something else to do. You're a smart person."

"We can't go back to New York."

"Why not?"

"I don't have a job. I don't want to go back. I'm sick of the city."

"We don't fit in here. We're poor and everyone else is rich."

"Not everyone."

"Isn't it weird to be a working man in a resort town?"

"I know. Lo how the mighty have fallen."

"I hate New England," she said. "People are so up-tight. Everything has to be just so. We're never going to crack the social crust here."

"You're probably right. I feel like I'm in exile. Do you still miss your family?" Doreen's parents and several of her siblings had moved to "Taos," and they had been out to visit them.

"Yes."

"We could move to Taos."

Tears came into her eyes. "Are you serious?"

Apparently he was. "You know how much I love Taos. I have had some kind of mystic relationship with Taos ever since the first time I went there, with Marco. I always go back. It's karma that your parents moved there. I can be Bruno's representative in New Mexico and build harpsichords. I can find something to do. Your father will help us."

"Really? Can we?"

"I don't see why not. We're not getting anywhere here."

"We should move before the baby comes."

"Well yes, we should. We always seem to move clear across the country when you're pregnant. I like it. We can start another new life."

And there we went. Movers came and took everything away, and we piled into the Mustang and hit the road again. As we drove out of town I heard Doreen say, "I hope I never set eyes on this place again."

David said, "I second that," and I fuzzed out

73

behind the weird blue pill.

Chapter 6

The house outside Taos was one big room over another, crudely built, carved into a hillside a few miles south of town, but the high clear bright air made everything possible again. Doreen went right to work setting up her kitchen downstairs and making curtains for the upstairs windows. They brought in a big old-fashioned wood-gas cookstove and hooked it up to the chimney. David started fixing up the grungy lower room, covering over the dark paneling with fresh bright boards, building in a little room for Joey, reconstructing the bathroom with a tub for Doreen in place of the rusty, smelly old shower. They planted a lawn in the former dog yard and built raised beds for a vegetable garden.

It was a new life for me, that's for sure. The doors were often wide open and I came and went freely. Outside the kitchen was the big dirt flat where Doreen got David to rototill the beds for her garden. Beyond were two ponds connected by a little rivulet with a bridge across it, beyond them trees along the creek and fields beyond with scattered haystacks and adobe dwellings, below a backdrop of majestic mountains under an enormous sky. I sat on the upstairs deck and marveled. A small flock of huge white geese lived at the far end of the further pond. They came to visit most afternoons and took baths right in front of the house, splashing around in the water beside the bridge, squawking and squabbling, and one by one or all at once reared up wildly flapping their widespread wings to shake them dry. I decided not to mess with the geese.

There were also chickens, over toward the other house, in a shed of their own with a large wire outdoor cage where they wandered around all day in complete confusion, jerking their heads at each other and pecking at the ground. I could sit and watch them for hours, cocking my head and trying to detect a pattern in their incessant movement, but it made no sense at all. They were really hopelessly stupid.

A bigger challenge was the onset of Doreen's dog Floppy, whom her mother had been keeping for her for the past few years. Doreen had acquired another dog in Stonington, Fred, but he was useless and didn't last long. Fred was not hostile, happily, but he had no interest in anything but running around, not caring that it made endless trouble for our people. The last straw was when he went up the aisle to the altar in the Catholic church on the town square during Easter morning mass. Goodbye Fred.

Floppy was a different story. Only her ears were floppy. The rest of her was buff, brown on top, with dirty white legs and belly and white patches on her chest and face. She knew some other cats and treated me nicely from the start. I hissed her at first, but just a little, to make the point, and then we were cool. She kept busy most of the day, off chasing geese or poking around in the high grass, doggily, or out in the yard with Doreen and Joey. She had more or less forgotten Doreen, but slowly it was coming back. They developed or redeveloped some kind of bond, maybe female; which made it all the clearer that David was my person, and vice versa, which was fine with me. We were starting to understand each other. I liked that.

David and Doreen loosened up with each other too. Maybe they were right about New England. David stayed home all day so he could spell her with Joey, who had to be watched every minute and played with a certain amount, and they had much more time together. Doreen grew an enormous vegetable garden, tomatoes falling every which way; David grew marijuana plants six feet tall behind a wooden fence. She was more and more pregnant and the coming child drew them into closer alignment.

The house improvements were done, with a new bookcase wall screening off their bed in the big room upstairs. David built a wooden crib that hung from the rafters on chains beside the bed. The nights were getting chilly, and they laid in a pile of piñon wood for the upstairs and downstairs stoves.

Doreen started feeling contractions one morning after breakfast. Her mother came over and picked up Joey and took him to Gramma's house. David gave himself to her and they quietly enjoyed the passing hours, drinking tea in the kitchen and sitting together on the swing he had put up downstairs. As the light faded the contractions grew stronger; he helped her climb the stairs and installed her on the sofa. He built up a fire in the stove, turned on lights, pulled the curtains. He scrambled an egg. Tess the midwife came. Doreen's doctor father showed up with her sister Susie and a tank of oxygen. It was a slow day but the actual birth was fast and dramatic, with a last-minute crisis narrowly averted. The baby was limp and bluish purple until Susie suctioned its airway and did some other tricks that got it breathing. Then it was fine, another vigorous boy, another irreplaceable rush of major joy.

Nobody paid any attention to me. I had to remind David to give me my dinner. After I ate I went out under the starry moonless sky, feeling oddly at home on the planet.

·

As the winter took hold they were more inclined to go to bed early and lay around longer in the morning. I slept downstairs with Joey, who was not happy to be down there by himself. One of them came down every night and read to him and sweetly lay with him until he went to sleep, and I stayed on for extra warmth. When the light came we went up and he crawled in with his mommy and daddy and the baby, all snuggly together, while I lay close to Floppy on the foot of the bed, possibly even touching if the air was cold.

David was writing for the local paper and directing plays again, going out to rehearsal many nights. It was hard for Doreen. The winter was harsh, fierce winds blowing in off the mesa and sucking the heat out of the house. The wood was hard to split and wet and wouldn't burn. At first she liked chopping wood, getting her strength back; later she hated it. The two boys needed constant attention. She wanted to make art.

"David," she said at the breakfast table the Sunday after the season's second show opened, "please don't do any more shows for a while. Please. I know you're a tremendous hit right now and probably can do anything you want, but I need you here. Stay here. I'll give you time to write. I need you."

"We may have an order for a harpsichord," he said. "I got a letter yesterday from some people in Albuquerque asking for a quote. I said five thousand."

"That would help."

"I have to pay three thousand for the parts, but still."

"Isn't that an awfully low price?"

"I don't know. It seemed like a lot to me. I am also getting the tech director job at the auditorium, I think. We have to have some money coming in. I only have to go in when something is happening. The newspaper is ridiculous. Other than that I will stay home and make a harpsichord."

"Thank you."

"I want to be home. I hate going away from you and our sweet little boys. Maybe I will write a play. I'd like to do one of my own next year."

"I'm so glad to hear you say that. You're you again," she said. "Working for Bruno was beating you down."

"I know, but it paid the rent. I'm going to start baking more bread and trading it for goat's milk, isn't that a good idea? I met this guy who keeps goats on the ranch across the road. I love goat's milk. And what about you? Don't you want to paint?"

"I'm going to a life class with Mother on Saturday morning, next Saturday, is that all right?"

"I have to go in and do a setup. I can take Joey with me. He'll like it."

"I need help with the garden, too."

"I'll help you."

"More milk," said Joey for the umpteenth time, banging his cup on the table.

"Joey, please, for heaven's sake," said David, "just ask, don't demand. You can have milk as long as there's milk."

"Give me more milk."

"May I have some more milk," said David, going to the refrigerator.

"Want milk?"

"All right, you get the idea, take your time," David said, pouring milk. I meowed and he gave me some too.

•

The harpsichord order came through. Now that the weather was starting to warm up he could work on it in the flimsy glass-house off the kitchen, which was useless as a solar collector. The parts came in boxes from Stonington, and he put them together from instructions he had helped to write. The work went well when the weather cooperated, but there were many days when it was too cold in the shop, and other things needed to be done, gigs at the auditorium and the newspaper, the garden, small boys to entertain. By summer the body of the instrument was done, and Doreen had painted intricate blue borders and bouquets of flowers on the soundboard, mixing her pigments with egg yolk. but the keyboard was only half finished, the stringing and fiddly work yet to be begun.

Meanwhile David's former life had reached out to him again, and he had accepted an invitation to direct and teach at a summer theatre festival in southern California. He wrapped up his obligations and was all set to go, but as the moment approached, one sensed that something was not quite right about the plan. One afternoon I came upon him standing in the warm rain gazing at the rainbow across the valley, green fields bright in the sunlight, mountains dark behind.

"This is real," he told me. I already knew.

The day before his planned departure he came back from town and announced, "I'm not going," even before he came down the stairs. Doreen was not in the kitchen. He found her out in the sunny backyard doing laundry at their classic machine, running clothes through the wringer, ready to hang them on the line. Sam lay on his face on a quilt thrown down on the long silky grass. Joey came running at him, wearing a feathered war bonnet, with red lines painted on his cheeks, crying, "Daddy!" and David scooped him up and hugged him and whirled him around. "I'm not going," he said again.

"What do you mean?"

"I'm not going. I'm staying here."

"Really?"

"How can I leave this? It's so beautiful here. I love being here with you and Joey and Sammy and Charles, it is heaven on earth. It makes no sense to spend Taos's best month in the baking hot polluted San Bernardino Valley, it sounds horrible. What was I thinking?"

"You said you would go."

"I know, I know. Murray pushed me. He made it a matter of honor or maleness or art. Something I needed to do. It would be a cop-out not to. He's right. And I wanted to do it, theoretically. I love Murray, I love his work, and it means a lot to me that he respects me and accepts me as an artist. I was flattered. Why is it always a choice between life and art? I want both!"

"You'll have a good time."

"I'm not going. I already called them. I can't leave now. Too bad about my theatre career, which is not happening anyway. My last play in New York was a nightmare. I told them I have to work on the harpsichord. And I do. We need the money. They were freaked out, but what could they say?"

"Yes, work on the harpsichord. I am so glad you're staying here. I was dreading your absence."

"Were you? I thought you wanted me to go."

"I thought you wanted to go and I should be brave."

"I'm going to be brave and stay home. I don't want to go anywhere. I don't want to talk to anyone or do anything or go into town. They all think I'm gone and we should keep it that way. I'm going away but staying here. I'm not answering the phone. If anyone calls, tell them I'm in California. "

"Are you serious?"

"Absolutely." He threw himself down in the grass with Sam and Joey and lay on his back with the two boys crawling over him. "I am so happy," he said to the sky.

"So am I," she said, bending down and kissing him and patting his head.

•

What is there to say about happiness? Every moment is full of it, every movement fully felt. I am there basically all the time, it is my norm as long as other animals don't fuck it up.

"I adore not going into town," David said, sitting at the kitchen table closely inspecting and polishing harpsichord keys one at a time. "I am completely happy out here on the ranch, but as soon as I go into town things get complicated.

People come at me with attitudes or ideas and I have to respond. I can't think, I can't pursue any purpose of my own, I just ricochet from one crazy person to another. I don't want to do that."

"What are you going to do?"

"I would make another harpsichord if I had another order. I'd like to do another play. I could do one a year maybe? I am writing one."

"What is it about?"

"It's a translation, a Spanish classic."

"You don't know Spanish."

"I have a dictionary, and three bad translations. I am rewriting it. I am writing poetry. I am writing high language like Shakespeare. It's a thrill!"

"Is there a part for me?"

"Yes, there's a fabulous part for you. And a part for your father. Do you think he will do it?"

"Probably, but I am not ready yet," she said. "We have to wait till Sammy is a little older."

"I thought we would do it in the winter. First I have to finish this harpsichord and then I have to get a job. We are totally broke."

"How close are you?"

"I will have it playing in a couple of days. Then I need to play it for a while. It will be ready to deliver by the end of August. That will pay the rent anyway."

They set the new harpsichord up in the yard to photograph it. I posed with it. It was dark blue with gold leaf bands and gold leaf around the keyboard with elaborate lettering in Latin. Doreen did the decoration. David had only played on it for a few days when the owners suddenly pounced, arriving unexpectedly from Albuquerque with a van. They admired the instrument without seriously playing it or seeming to appreciate how much work it represented, paid for it, and took it away.

•

With it went the magic of the summer. Before we knew it the nights were cold and coming earlier.

"Guess what," said David, who had called Stonington and talked to his former boss, who knew all there was to know about harpsichords.

"What?"

"Bruno informs me that my dear customers sold the harpsichord for nine thousand dollars. They didn't even have it for two weeks. They weren't taking it to California, it was a scam. I feel like a complete idiot."

"Shit!" she said.

"I thought they were a little weird. I tried to be friendly to them but there was nothing there. They don't even play."

"I thought she did."

"No. She plays the piano."

"Did you get diapers?"

"Bill will pay me tomorrow." David was working for an actor friend building a dome. "I know I shouldn't be working for four dollars an hour but it's all he can afford. I love doing it, building a house from the ground up, it's totally cool. We'll be all right. There are some shows coming into the auditorium, I'll have some hours."

But it wasn't cool in November, when the days turned dark and the wind came up the canyon. The ground turned into mud and then froze. David came home filthy and exhausted, and the house was chilly.

"I'm sorry," Doreen said. "Joey was sick and throwing up, and I was trying to teach Sam the letters, and then it was getting dark, and I just didn't go out and chop wood."

"I'll do it," he said grimly.

"I'm sorry."

"Don't be sorry. There's no reason you should have to split all the wood. It's too much."

He went out and came back in a while with an armload of wood. He set to work making a fire in the stove.

"If I could just have a little help…"

"I help you," he said. "I'm doing the best I can. I have to work. I like building a house but it isn't easy."

"Are you suggesting that I don't work?"

"No, of course you do. You work all the time. You're a hero. I'll be home after this week. We finished closing it in today. It was beautiful when it was open and the sun was shining through the bones. Now it's dark inside and depressing, plywood and dirt, and seems smaller. We're going to wrap it up for the season. They don't have any more money and it's too cold to work outside."

"I need to get out of here," she said. "I never go anywhere or see anyone." What was she talking about? I was there. Two little kids were there, and sometimes another one came over and played. She and the other mommy traded intimacies over pots of tea and only intervened when the children squabbled. Floppy curled up by the stove. It couldn't have been cozier.

"Are you all right?"

"No," she said. "I feel ugly and fat. You don't

love me anymore."

"Now now," he said, putting his arms around her. "I love you. I do. You are beautiful to me."

"I'm not eating. Can you feed the boys?"

"You should eat. It's winter, you need fuel to keep warm. I'll make spaghetti."

"I'm going into town."

"What for?"

"Give me the keys." He gave them to her.

"I wish you wouldn't go off like this. I feel like something else is going on. We were in the middle of a conversation."

"I'll be back." She went up the stairs. David stood there listening to her put her coat and boots on. She told Joey and Sam their daddy was making dinner and they should go to bed and not wait up for her. We heard her go out the door, get into the car, and drive away. I went outside with David while he chopped some more wood. The night was still, silent, icy, the sky glittering with stars, so clear you could see them suspended in space. The wood was coated in ice, the pieces too big for the cookstove, resistant to splitting. He couldn't do it and stopped and looked at the stars, and at me, and thought, then went at it again until he had a reasonable stack of wood and took it in.

Chapter 7

There was a snowstorm, and then another, bigger, and the snow melted in the bright winter sun, and that left the driveway so deep in mud they were afraid to drive in. So they parked the car up on the county road that cut across the hillside above the house. They were going into town to rehearsals five nights a week, dropping the boys off with babysitters on the way, picking them up after, carrying them asleep into the house and popping them into their beds. There was a huge snowstorm, and Doreen's mother lent them her Blazer, which had four-wheel drive, so they could get around.

The next time David went to start the Mustang the battery was dead. When he went back the next day to get the battery and take it into town, someone had smashed in the rear window. The back seat was littered with broken glass and snow was blowing in, their once nifty little car looking pitiful and betrayed. The day after that, I was up on the hill at a place I like to go and was surprised to see three young guys get out of a pickup truck and look at the car very interestedly. One of them wriggled in through the back window and popped the hood and they had a good look at the engine, nodding and pumping fists and doing special handshakes. Rigging a long rope from the front of the Mustang to the hitch on their truck, they towed it away. It was over quickly. My people didn't come back until much later and David didn't notice till the next day.

"I don't believe it," he said, coming in and stamping his feet. "What a disaster!"

"What happened?"

"It's gone. It's not there. Our car been stolen. I don't believe it."

"What are you going to do?"

"Call the sheriff, I guess."

"They'll find it. We'll get it back."

"I hope so."

Before he could do anything he received a call that cheered him up.

"Guess what. Bill saw them towing it down the road. He recognized our car and followed them and got their license number. I wish he had followed them home but he was going the other way. If I can find out where they live, maybe I can just go get it. If I just show up, they probably will let me take it back, if I can get it to run. We can't exist here without a car."

"You should call the sheriff."

"I don't want to get law enforcement involved if we can help it. He said they probably want it for the engine. It's some kind of legendary engine."

"Great."

The upshot was that they got some money from the parents of the boys who had stolen the car, which was no longer functional, and they were so broke they had to spend it on living expenses. The winter was half over, but they couldn't live in the country without a car, and Doreen's mother needed her Blazer. David called Bruno and talked his way back into a job at the harpsichord factory. The play opened and was more or less a fiasco, I gathered, and it was goodbye to Taos. Doreen packed up the kitchen once again. David rented a big truck, and a couple of theatrical friends helped him load it up. We were all sad.

David had started painting the walls of the big room upstairs before Christmas and not quite finished it, and the last night, when most of their stuff was in the truck parked outside, he stayed up late to do the rest.

"Why are you doing that?" Doreen demanded. "You should come to bed."

"I want to finish. I don't want to leave it unfinished. It's such a beautiful color, pale lavender that will change color with the changing light, bright in the daytime and warm at night."

"You're crazy."

"I'm not ready to go to sleep so I might as well finish painting. I've never been so exhausted. I'm sick but can't give in to it. I'm going on nerve. I can sleep in Kansas. Once we're in Kansas I'll be all right."

"Are you going to be well enough to drive?"

"Totally. I am looking forward to the road trip."

"I'm not."

"It will be wonderful to be all together for a few days, just us, the nuclear family, in the cab of the truck. We never spend any time together, we're always running off for various reasons, flying apart—"

"All you have to do is drive."

"You can drive."

"I don't want to."

"Good, because I do. Did you talk to Alicia? Can we stay with them for a couple of weeks? Can we put our stuff in Stefan's mother's barn until we find a place? I have to take the truck back as soon as we get there. Every extra day costs some outlandish amount."

"I think so."

"You don't sound very definite. I have to go to work immediately. You'll have to find us an apartment. We have to tread water until I get paid."

"How do you feel about going back?"

"I'm O.K. with it," he said. "I love Taos but there's no market for harpsichords in New Mexico, what was I thinking? There's no money in Taos unless you're a dynamic entrepreneurial type who can make money in any situation, which unfortunately I am not. We have to have some cash flow. I can be useful there, and Bruno needs you. He doesn't have anyone else to paint his soundboards." David finished painting and turned around admiring the empty room. They were leaving the shelves. "Isn't it beautiful?" he said. "Let's go to bed."

"What are we going to do with Charles? Put him in the back?"

"His box can go on the floor in front of the passenger seat. We can pad it up and make a flat platform for you and the boys. It will be nicer than sitting up on the seat."

"I'm going to miss Floppy."

"She'll be fine with your mother. She wouldn't want to be cooped up in an apartment."

"You're right."

"You can get another dog."

Oh great! Floppy was harmless but you never know with dogs.

∙

Stupefied days alternated with more or less lucid nights in a succession of motel rooms. Doreen was sick of the boys by the time we stopped for the night and withdrew into the bathtub with a book while David roughhoused with his two sons, who were still full of energy and fun, bouncing on the two big beds and practicing stunts, balancing on David's feet as he lifted them up, crying, "Superboy!" He got down on the floor with them and "roughed them up," saying, "Rough, rough, rough," in a rough voice, scratching and kneading their backs and bodies with a playful roughness that made them laugh and scream with pleasure.

The last day they didn't drug me, which was a relief—I hated that blahed-out useless feeling—and I restrained myself pretty well, moaning a little but not too loudly. David pulled the blanket back from one end of my box so I could see him up above me driving the truck, looking strong and serious. That made it bearable.

When we got out we were at Stefan's mother's farm. I had been there before for a picnic when the lilacs were in bloom and everything was perfect. This time it was dreary, the day gray and chilly, the ground spongy outside the shed where they unloaded the truck, their battered furniture looking sad and lifeless. Then we got back in. They left the dreaded box with the rest of the stuff and let me ride loose.

"You have to sit still," David told me. "You can't climb around on my neck, it's too hard to drive. Can he sit on your lap? Sam, you can go down on the floor, see what that's like. We're almost there."

"I'll be so glad to get out of this truck," Doreen said.

"I don't know," David said. "I'm almost sorry it's over. I was just getting into it. Do you remember any of this, Joey? You were little when we left."

"I don't know," Joey said, but when we came up over the viaduct into the village he suddenly knew where he was. "I know this," he said. "That's the harpsichord factory. I walked over this bridge with my babysitter."

"I don't know," Doreen said. "Maybe this is a mistake."

"Are you seriously saying that, right now, at this very moment?"

"Don't bite my head off."

"I'm not. But I do think we need a positive attitude."

"Where are we going?" Joey said.

"It smells funny down here," Sam said. He tried to climb up onto the seat between David and Joey, but Joey blocked him with his knees and pushed him up against the dashboard. I climbed up onto the back of the seat and lay down, and Joey flopped over onto Doreen's lap.

"Sit up, Joey," she said. "I can't take any more contact. Please!"

"We're going to the Ludwigs' house. We're going to stay with them until we find a house of our own. They are a lot of fun but you have to really be good so we can all get along. Just remember that it's their house. We have to fit in with whatever is going down and not try to have our own way. Can you do that? It's just for a little while. It's like a house party. We'll get our own life back."

"I'm so tired," Doreen said.

"How do you think I feel? I drove two thousand miles. You've just been sitting there."

"Be nice."

"I think you're wonderful. We made it. Here we are."

The house was crowded. I stayed under the bed in David and Doreen's room because there were other cats around that I didn't want to deal with. Rose moved in with Lily, her big sister, so Joey and Sam could sleep in her bed. Joey got along with Lily but Rose bit Sam, which began a series of hysterical spats. Doreen tried to be nice, but when her child was attacked, whoever was at fault, she was a demon, and Alicia didn't take it sitting down. David was off at work all day. Stefan was out in his studio in the garage welding. When they came in they found the children locked up in various separate rooms and the women furious with each other. They all calmed down and made dinner and the next day was not so bad.

The floors were wood painted gray.

"We can't stay here," Doreen whispered to David when they were in bed.

"I know. I think I have a place," he murmured. "My mother is talking to Mrs. Dickinson, you remember, where we had martinis when my parents came to visit, they have two houses and they're not even here, they won't be back for a couple of months."

"Can we move tomorrow?"

"We can't push but it just might happen."

"I hope so. I wish Alicia would talk to Rose but she says it's all Sam's fault. Don't do that."

"Why not?" he whispered. "Don't you want to make love? It's been days. What's the matter?"

"They can hear us."

"So what? Love is good. Kiss me."

"Shhh."

"I'll be quiet," he whispered.

They were quiet, but of course I could hear them, they were right on top of me, and I was glad. The love thing always made them happier.

•

Well it was very pleasant at Mrs. Dickinson's but she only let us stay a week and then we moved to another apartment that Doreen had acquired with enormous sturm und drang. I followed it as best I could. She spotted this place, the whole third floor of a big old house, ideally located in the middle of town, which was important because they didn't have a car. He could walk to work, she could shop, etc. But the owner's wife didn't want to rent to a family and turned her down. I was not the problem. Time was running out. David found a possible place on the edge of the next town, and they were all set to move in, starting to carry the refrigerator up the outside stairs, when Alicia told Doreen firmly, "You can't live here," and Doreen burst into tears. Of course she couldn't. David could carpool in to work but she and the boys would be stuck. So they put the refrigerator back on the truck, and Doreen confronted the resistant landlady again with two perfect children by her side and begged, and the woman gave in, and we moved.

More wood floors, worn and reasonably warm, and they settled in as if we were going to stay. Is this the way they like to live, moving and moving again, setting up a house and then taking it apart and setting it up somewhere else, and again? I hated it but in a way I liked it. I hated being uprooted just when I fully understood the immediate geography and came to an understanding with the fauna. At the same time, it was exciting to cast off again not knowing where we would land. Anything could happen.

•

Doreen's sister Susie came for Christmas, finding a particularly warm welcome because she had a car. Having another person around was more fun, although Doreen and Susie got mad at each other a lot. I was an inside cat again, which was O.K. with me. There were plenty of rooms and places to go, including a cupola up a steep stair where David sometimes escaped to smoke and write. I went with him and helped, but it was often too cold up there. He didn't get much time to himself.

Susie said, "I'd like to stay and study dance at Connecticut College this term, is that a good idea? Can I stay here?"

"I like having you here," David said.

"Stay, stay," Sam said.

"Stay, please," Joey said, drowning him out.

"The boys want you to. It helps Doreen, I know. It's nice that you have a car and we can go to the movies once in a while."

"Am I expected to cook for you and do your laundry?" Doreen said from the stove.

"Of course not."

"Why are you just sitting there?"

"I'm trying to keep out of your way."

"I'll get out of your way. Help yourselves. I

hope it's good," Doreen said and stomped out of the room and down the hall and slammed the bedroom door.

"What's that about?" David said.

"How would I know?" Susie said.

"It's not your fault," David said. "It's just the way she is. It's hard not to take it personally, but it isn't personal, no matter how much she thinks it is. You have to make up your mind to just take it. It's only part of the time. She's a wonderful person."

"I know that."

"Is she jealous of, you know, you and me?"

"I hope not. What a weird suggestion!"

"I am not suggesting anything. I just wondered."

"I can get a place in New London."

"No, please, stay, I mean it. I'm trying to settle down. It's been a rough couple of years. Let's just be normal, can we? You're family, we have room, of course you should stay. Personally I like living in a big family."

"That's because you never did it."

"Oh, cut it out. Your family is terrific. You have fun. Some of those parties at your parents' house were outrageous."

"I miss them."

"But you want a little distance. I understand."

"Just for a couple of months. Then I'll go back."

•

In the event she stayed for a whole year. The summer was unbearably hot up in our mansard attic, the slanting walls radiating heat that built up all day and didn't dissipate till the middle of the night, the humans sweating although practically naked. Before the following winter, the downstairs neighbor moved out leaving the rooms unheated; as a result, cold came up through the floor instead of warmth. Doreen was depressed and ate a lot and got fat, then went on a diet and got thin and complained of having no energy. David picked on her for not being more fun, but it turned out she was sick. She recovered but they were still on the outs, arguing and suffering month after month for no good reason. Sometimes she would go to bed and put a pillow over her head and leave David to cope. Susie was seldom there and didn't really participate. David felt trapped in a humiliating job, desperate to express himself, and elaborated one escape fantasy after another—write a tv series, go back to newspaper work, open a café theatre. Doreen egged him on but it was totally impractical: they still didn't even have a car. He had to keep working for Bruno; it would take months to pay off their credit cards and dig themselves out of the hole they had fallen into. In the meantime life was rather grim.

"Are you mad at me?"

"I am never mad at you," he said, but it was not exactly true. They were both thrashing around in some kind of general dissatisfaction, which came in waves. The boys were freaked out by it. Then periodically they would break through and laugh and make love and relax for a while and be happy again. It didn't last, though.

None of this bothered me particularly, but I was sorry they were having a hard time.

Chapter 8

Susie flew back to New Mexico for Christmas and stayed, leaving her car until a brother-in-law could come and get it. David and Doreen had some new friends, Rolf Schmidt, a tall phlegmatic German newly employed at the harpsichord shop, and his wife, Beth, a California girl, who was extremely talkative and friendly. I disclose herewith that I had a special relationship with Beth, a big woman who simply overwhelmed me with love. Normally I am a dignified cat and rather easily offended. Beth, unlike anyone else I have ever known, ignored my defenses, lifted me right up to her face, laughing at my attempts to defend myself, nuzzled me, cooing ridiculously, and had the temerity to turn me over on my back in her lap and scratch my tummy—and I let her do it, over and over. What a feeling!

The Schmidts didn't know anyone in Stonington so David invited them over for dinner. Beth started coming over to have tea with Doreen while the men were at work. Then gradually they started being there for dinner every night. Two more at the table seemed to make things easier. Rolf's English was limited and he rarely said anything, though he seemed to follow what was said; Beth talked enough for two people. Doreen seemed excited by their presence.

After dinner David put the boys to bed in the bunk beds he had built for them, reading fairy tales to them once they were in their pajamas, turning the light out and lying in bed with one and then the other until all was calm. When he came back into the kitchen the others were still at the table talking. He washed the dishes and sat down for a while. It seemed like they could go on all night. He eventually said it was his bedtime and withdrew.

"Are they going to come over for dinner every night?" David asked when Doreen finally came to bed. "I feel like I need some time off."

"It isn't every night," she said.

"Well, practically every night. They've been here the last three nights in a row, and they were here on Saturday and several days last week."

"Are you keeping track?"

"I keep track of everything."

"Oh leave me alone."

"I like them fine, but they're not the most interesting people in the world. I'd like to maybe read, or talk to you."

"Don't you know what's going on?"

"Do I want to?"

"You don't love me."

"I do. I adore you," he said. "Don't attack me. You're not sleeping with Rolf, are you? He's not your type. He's certainly not my type, ha ha."

But she was. They had chased me off the bed and done it that very afternoon while the babysitter took the boys out for a walk. They didn't care that I knew because I couldn't tell.

Now David knew it too.

"I wish you wouldn't," he said.

"I can't go on like this. Don't you understand? "

"Like what? I'm not telling you what to do or not to do, I want you to be happy, I'm just saying I wish you wouldn't. I want you for me and our little unit."

"He's not taking anything away from you."

"Well, that's good."

"I can love more than one person."

"I'm sure you can."

"Stop being so positive."

"Do you want me to be jealous? Sorry, I don't think I want to play that game. I don't want anybody but you, but if I did, I'd probably want to be free to pursue it, within reason, so what can I say? Be cool. Don't destroy us."

"My idea is that we should get a house together."

"And I suppose you want me to sleep with Beth. That would make things much easier for you, wouldn't it."

"Yes, you should."

"But I don't want you sleeping with Rolf, I want you sleeping with me. I want to be married. I want to be married to you. I don't want all this other confusion. My wild days are long in the past. Oh right, you're ten years younger than I am. Right."

"No, you should do it to give her a baby," she said. "They want a baby and they can't do it because his sperm is not viable or something, I don't know exactly. It would be a tremendous gift."

"Do we have to move in with them?"

"I'll die," she said. "Do you want me to die?"

"Aren't you being a little melodramatic?"

"I'm talking about my feelings. Don't criticize my style."

"Don't get mad. Whatever you want, my darling, my precious beloved. Just don't take yourself away from me. I want you, I want you to be happy."

"We have to move," she said. "We're going to asphyxiate ourselves heating with the Glenwood. We need a yard. Together we can afford a house. I want a dog. I want a garden. I want the boys to go outside and play. I've been so unhappy here."

"I know. Believe me. I'm doing my best."

"I know you are."

"All right. It's probably a good idea. The nuclear family is a nightmare. I prefer communal living. I'll think about the other. I don't know quite how to broach it."

"We can all go to bed together," she said.

So that's what they did a few nights later, after the boys were well asleep. I got trapped in with the grownups when they closed the bedroom door. Ignoring me, they hugged in a standing clump, as they had done sometimes before, wrapping their arms around each other and pressing together. They lit a candle and all got naked in the semidark and got into the bed, two pairs kissing and cooing, and then the usual extended thrashing and squirming, doubled. I escaped when Beth got up and went into the bathroom.

•

They found a suitable house in another town a few miles away; David could ride to work with Rolf. The house had tall white pillars on the front, a large sunny side yard, and an enormous copper beech tree out back. Doreen requisitioned one of the two parlors for her studio, and David took a little room off it for his writing. The dining room had a bay window at one end, and the kitchen was commodious. Upstairs, the Schmidts had the room in the front, Doreen and David had the room in the back, and Joey and Sam shared a big room in between. It was a much better setup.

And the atmosphere greatly improved. There were more people to pay attention to the boys so Doreen didn't feel so trapped. The four adults took turns making dinner and tried to equitably share the housework. There were regular group hugs, but they generally slept with their own partners, less often pairing up the other way. The ménage was civilized and mellow, especially on evenings when Rolf and Beth, both skilled recorder players, joined David to play baroque chamber music while Doreen painstakingly laid down egg tempera decorations on a harpsichord soundboard in the other room.

She also painted a series of still lifes and portraits in egg on wood panels that Rolf made for her at the shop and David gessoed. She was excited again about being an artist. David got up early most days, ahead of everyone else, and sequestered himself in his study as long as he could; he was writing a novel, but I don't think he told anyone but me.

A friend of Rolf's came from Germany, bought a rickety Toyota to tour the U.S., and sold the car to David and Doreen before he went home; then the women were no longer stuck when the men drove off to work.

In the spring Rolf's parents came to visit. Beth made them a comfortable nest in the attic, and they stayed for a month, playing Oma and Opa to the friendly boys. Doreen acquired a kitten, which was a bit of a brat but no threat to me; I was kind of sorry when it ate poison and died on the way to the vet. Beth set up a loom and was teaching David how to weave.

After a while Beth was pregnant, she and Rolf were happy about that, and David too, but Doreen was getting twisted. She and Alicia put henna on their heads, which was fun but turned Doreen's normally straight dark hair reddish and frizzy. Everybody pretended to like it, but as it grew out it lost its novelty. Then she cut her hair radically short, which made her look boyishly fierce and desperate. For days she stared intently into a mirror, painting a portrait of herself that seemed to be obsessing and upsetting her. I wished I could understand art but I can no more look at a picture than I can read a book. Doreen and David both tried to show me, holding me up in front of one picture in particular, saying, "Look, it's you," but I didn't get it. They evidently see more than I do. To me paintings look like flat blobs of random colors. I don't know why they hang them on the walls or how they can get so worked up about them.

"I hate this picture more and more,"

Doreen said one night, standing in the harsh light of the fluorescent tubes David had put up over her drawing board, glaring at the panel propped up on her easel. The other three were kicking back in the softly lit living room talking about playing music but too full of dinner to do it. Sam was sitting on Rolf's lap flipping through a picture book. I was on Beth's.

"What's the matter with it?" David said. "I think it's beautiful."

"I hate the way I look."

"I think you look wonderful. I love you with short hair," David said, rising and moving into the light. "It makes you more visible. You can see the bones and shapes. It gives you a different presence, more vivid and provocative. I think you should keep it this way."

"I can't paint. I'll never be an artist. This is shit."

"Why are you saying that?" he said. "Stop it right now. This is the best work you've ever done, and you know it. I love this one."

"Don't look at it," she said, blocking his view. "I mean it." He went back and sat down. I slipped away from Beth and climbed up next to him on the sofa.

"Why don't you take a break?" he said. "Come. Let's play hearts. I'll put the boys to bed and then we'll play. It takes at least four. You don't have to work all the time. Have some fun."

"I don't want to have fun," Doreen said, brandishing a large screwdriver at the painting on the easel.

"What are you doing?" I could feel him shaking. She scratched several long gouges across the painting with the end of the screwdriver. He practically jumped out of his skin. "Doreen, for God's sake!"

"I don't care," she said. "I just don't care. Fuck you all." Putting down the screwdriver, she glared at them, wiped her hands on a rag, and went out the other way. The outside door closed.

"What was that all about?" David said in a tight voice. The picture was still on the easel, brightly lit. "I can't look," he said. "It's like she killed something." Averting his eyes, he sidled into the studio and switched off the light, hesitated, started to go into his study, but instead came back to Sam and took him from Rolf, saying, "Come with me, sweetie, sleepy time, I'll read you a story," and carried him up the stairs, the little boy confidently putting his arms around his father's neck.

"Is she mad at me?" Beth asked when she and Rolf and I were alone. "I don't know what I have done or not done."

"It's me," he said. "It is I. That sounds never right."

"Never sounds right. Nobody says that. Don't worry about it. Möchtest du Deutsches sprechen?"

"No."

"Your English is getting very good."

"It is better. I understand what people say. I can't quickly talk. Bruno is excited and talks so fast I can't keep up."

"Is it a problem?"

"No."

"Did you hurt her feelings?"

"I did, maybe."

"Why? What's the matter?"

"Well, you're pregnant, it's different, don't you think?"

"David wants to sleep with me anyway. He says it's important for the child. He says he puts his spirit into it when he comes, it's magical, some esoteric substance passes."

"Please, spare me."

"He's very sweet! It's good. Love is good. You're not responsible for Doreen's moods. They're not about you, they're internal. You're not a woman, you can't possibly understand. You are not the problem. She'll work it out."

"I want to love the baby. I want to be with you. Let's go to bed." They got up and started turning off lights.

"Leave a light on for Doreen," she said.

"I hope she's all right."

"David is coming back down, unless he falls asleep with the boys. Probably not. He's freaked out because she's freaked out. She will calm down and come back. Don't worry, be happy." They went up.

A while later David came down and went into his study. I followed him and rubbed against his legs, and he absently scratched my head. I settled in the sling chair. He switched on the radio, sat at his desk, smoked a joint, and wrote with his fountain pen for a long time in his big black notebook. It was extremely peaceful. I like that feeling best, when everything is in balance, when we are quietly together and nothing else is happening.

•

"I think you should go away," David said to Doreen a few days later when the boys had gone with Rolf and Beth to the farmers' market and they had the house to themselves.

"It's my house too," she said.

"Of course it is, but you're not happy, you're mad at Beth all the time."

"I am sick of cleaning up after her. She's a pig. I don't know how you can stand to touch her."

"You don't have to clean up after her. You don't anyway. What are you talking about?"

"I can't wait to get away from them."

"Isn't that a little ironic? You were the one who wanted to live with them. You insisted on it, if you recall. You can go up to the cabin. It's heavenly there this time of year. Go for a week, be by yourself, let it all go. There's too much pressure here, I see how it is. Then when you get back it will almost be time to look for a house of our own. The year is almost up. They want their own place for the baby. I don't blame them."

"No, you blame me."

"There is no blame."

"I don't want to be there by myself. The nights are too dark."

"You can light candles."

"I'll be scared to death."

"There is nothing to be afraid of. Jean-Pierre is right down the hill if you want company. You need to get away. I'm not trying to get rid of you, but frankly everything is cool here except you. I would like nothing better than a week to myself but I have to work. Maybe I will go when you get back."

"I don't think so," she said.

"You don't think so what?"

"Oh never mind. I'm sorry. You're right. I've been awful. But every time I try to be nice to her she does something mean or says something that makes me mad again. I'll be good. Do you still love me?"

"Yes of course. I mean, yes I do. Why do you keep asking that? It isn't helpful. Don't I tell you I love you often enough? No one ever said I love you in my family. Well maybe my mother, I'm sure she did, and Grammie, but usually not in so many words. That's one of the precious things I learned from you, darling. You make it easy."

"Easy to say."

"And true. I love our life. I know I'm a little distracted. I am writing something, it's always on my mind. I am totally frustrated artistically, if I am permitted to say that. I am in exile here, trapped in wage-slavery, cut off from my peers and any possibility of doing my work. It's my own fault, and it's worth it, and I can't think of any way out except to keep writing. I'm a different person. Probably you're more disappointed than I am that we're not living in New York and going to the theatre all the time. I don't want to do that anymore."

"Well maybe I will go," she said.

"I think it would be good for you. You can paint all day."

"Can I take Charles?"

"You can't take animals on the train or bus."

"I will carry him in a basket over my arm. Nobody will know he is in there."

"What if he yowls? You know how he is."

"I'll give him a pill if I have to, but I think he has outgrown the need. He is a much more mature cat than he used to be."

"I've noticed that his whiskers are going gray."

"No, those white whiskers were always there. It's what makes him look so sparkly. I will feel better if I have him with me. Otherwise I don't think I can take it."

"Of course you can take Charles," he said, "if

it's all right with him."

So off we went to the cabin. The trip was not bad at all. She carried me over her arm in a picnic basket, holding the lid down with her elbow, reaching in to pet me when she could get away with it, murmuring reassurances. I had never been on a train before; it was cool. When we stopped she lugged me out back of the station and put me down, laying out some newspapers so I could poop, I think that was the idea, anyway I did, and she gave me some water, and then we got on a bus, another new experience. I was down on the floor for most of the bus ride because all the seats were full. Their friend Jean-Pierre met us in the village, put my box in the back seat of his SUV, and drove us up into the hills. That was the worst part of the trip. I hate cars.

No one had been to the cabin recently and the mice had moved in, which was highly entertaining for me; it was more than a party, it was a feast! Doreen's plan to paint pictures all day was frustrated by more or less continuous rain the whole week. She went out and painted anyway, letting the rain smudge and pale her watercolors, hoping it might be an artistic effect. A couple of evenings I tagged along when she hiked down the hill to Jean-Pierre's house for dinner. He and his cats are serious meditators; I am glad to know a few Buddhist cats. Then finally the sun came out, and David and the boys arrived for the weekend, and it was like old times.

Chapter 9

Rolf and Beth found their own house, and it was just us again. After weeks of looking, Doreen discovered what turned out to be everyone's favorite house in another town across the river in Rhode Island. David could ride to work with either of two co-workers who lived close by. The house was big but at first it had a creepy vibe, not having been properly lived in for thirty years, long used as a doctor's office and private hospital. Layers of ancient worn linoleum on the floors of the main rooms were tacked down with a thousand tacks; in the kitchen the floor was disintegrating, but the upstairs floors were nice wood. Floors are important to me. The house was in grotty condition, in short, but it had good bones.

"It feels almost like the houses I grew up in," David said. "Don't you like how we are gradually clawing our way back into the middle class?"

Before they could paint the walls they tackled the floors, which would have been too tedious if their precious friends hadn't come to help—Rolf and Beth, now eight months pregnant and useless; Alicia and Stefan Ludwig, still their best friends; and another pair of artists, Victor and Jill Ainsley, who lived in a loft a few blocks away. We were sort of camping out in the house at that point. They had pizza delivered. Victor offered me a bite. I wish I liked it, but really, ick, I'll stick to cat food. They drank beer and had a good time pulling tacks. Eventually, after some hours, they got them all, and the guys broke up the tough old linoleum and dragged it out to be hauled away.

David and Doreen painted the rooms "Navajo white," a break from the bright-colored walls of houses past, imagining it infused the rooms with the clear bright air of the American West they hadn't stopped missing. David rented a sander and did the downstairs floors, complaining but good at it now. Rolf helped David lay down plywood on the kitchen and pantry floors and tile them in big red and black squares—which set me off rather well.

The house was in a pleasant old-fashioned neighborhood, with big trees and neat front yards, but our backyard was grotesquely overgrown with weeds and vines. Decades of neglect had produced a wall of brambles ten feet high outside the back door forming an impenetrable thicket all the way to the back fence, completely engulfing a playhouse. Doreen wanted access to the park-like backyard of the friendly neighbors around the corner. She attacked the nightmarish hedge while David was at work and Joey was in school, bit by bit hacking it down, making piles of the viciously prickered branches, which they then trucked to the dump in Victor Ainsley's van. It took her a couple of months. She kept at it doggedly.

Speaking of which, she now had a dog. She fell in love with him in a pet shop window and persuaded David to buy him for her for her birthday, though they could ill afford it and it was months away. He was black and white like me, a toy fox terrier, fat and sausage-like when they first brought him home. By spring he had slimmed down and livened up, and Doreen had the backyard looking like any nice backyard, grassy, with a picnic table and a big stone fireplace she had found buried in the jungle. David called the little dog Torpedo but Doreen thought that was cruel, and once he recovered from his pet shop depression they renamed him Whirly because of the way he ran around in circles in the yard chasing his tail. It was very cute. Whirly and I came to be good friends. We liked to chase each other around, which was fun; I felt young again.

There was a certain lack of irony in the way he did it, but I could overlook that.

•

David and Doreen attended the home birthing of Beth's baby, a little girl, which I gathered did not go smoothly, requiring a late-night drive to the hospital on ice unusual for October and hours waiting in the lobby, outsiders not permitted further in. The Schmidts were less constantly part of our lives now but occasionally came to dinner. I was always glad to see them.

Life became unprecedentedly regular. It felt like we could live in that house forever, and I hoped we would. David went to work. Joey went to school. Sam stayed home with Doreen, who played with him when she wasn't painting or cooking or reading. She acquired a pasta machine and draped spaghetti all over the kitchen. She had a regular flow of harpsichords coming through the house, making oil paintings in between. Women friends came over for tea, a couple of them with little kids, one with a silly fluffy dog. Whirly was, well, whirly, but he was not silly.

David, wildly discontented at work again, entertained one escape fantasy after another. "I spoke to the editor at the *Denver Post*. Uncle Sam told me they are looking for a drama critic. I sent him my résumé. What do you think?"

"Denver? I don't know. None of my family are there anymore. What would I do?"

"We could do plays at the Changing Scene. You can dance. Whatever you want. There are a lot of groovy people in Denver. Don't you want to see your friends?"

"I don't know if they like me anymore. Julius is still furious because I didn't give back all his science fiction books. It's really not such a big deal. Charlotte had a major crush on you."

"Really? I never knew that. Anyway, it probably won't happen. Like the *Soho News*. Like the *Voice*. I have another idea. You know that little former church across from the park that looks like a Greek temple? Well I can't stop thinking it would make a very sweet theatre. The rent is quite reasonable. I would have to get maybe twelve thousand a year to support it, that doesn't seem like very much, it would be a wonderful addition to the community. We could do anything we wanted, have a gallery downstairs, bring friends up from New York. I wish I were more entrepreneurial. I might do it with Lewis Cotter."

They had seen Lewis Cotter act in a play on a barge in the river.

"He's very handsome," she said.

"Yes, I've noticed."

"Are you attracted to him?"

"Bruno is talking about starting a magazine that I would be the editor of, *Early Keyboards*, that's another possibility, probably more realistic."

"You sound completely frazzled."

"Do I?"

"Let's just stay home."

"I wish I could. I am buying half a canoe, with Victor. We can go canoeing in the river."

"I am perfectly contented," she said. "I just want to hold still."

"Really? Is that what's happening?"

"Is it all right?"

"Whatever makes you happy is what I want. I love to make love to you. I am thinking of joining the morris dancers. They seem to have fun."

"Don't they drink an awful lot of beer? You don't want to drink that much beer."

"You have a point."

"This could be a theatre," she said, waving her arms around, "and then we could just do it."

"What, in the living room? Oh, I see what

you mean, the audience could be in the living room, and the dining room could be the stage. We could put up a curtain in the archway. I've always wanted a curtain that rises and falls. We can do my new play. It's been sitting on the shelf for a year, I don't know what else to do with it. It's a wonderful play."

"Is there a part for me?"

"No. I'm sorry but I told you after the last one, I don't want to direct you in any more plays. You fought with the other women in the cast. You made me talk about it day and night. It was too painful. Anyway the character is you. If you played it, it wouldn't be fiction, it would be some kind of documentary, which would be too weird. I need you to paint the set."

"Please?"

"No. I'm sorry. I mean it."

She was mad at him about that for a few days but eventually got over it. He cast the play with friends and friends' friends, including Victor and Jill Ainsley, Jill playing Doreen's part, and Lewis Cotter, who had lived in New York and was a real actor. Joey wanted to be in it so David wrote him in as a second at the duel. It was a long play. They practiced several evenings in the living room while Doreen finished decorating a harpsichord in the dining room. She stitched up a large red velvet curtain and David rigged pulleys above the arch so it would go up and down. The last scene took place at dawn in Taos; Doreen made a huge backdrop painting on brown paper in poster paints of the sun rising behind the Sangre de Christo. I could almost see it.

David was afraid to ask his cast to learn the lines so they did it as a staged reading, twice in front of audiences, squeezing thirty people into the living room each time. I watched it the first time from Beth's lap on the sofa in the front row. The coolest part in my opinion was the makeup and costumes. Lewis, playing a ghost, wore a white suit and powdered his face white, which made him look eerie and amazing. Victor at one point was dressed up as a kind of cave man, smudged with dirt, half-naked in a fur girdle, baring a fang. The audience didn't know what to make of it but they liked it well enough and stuck around afterwards for the feast of good food Doreen and David had whipped up.

"How do you feel?" she asked him over breakfast the morning after it was all over.

"Good. Relieved. Let down. Tired. I can't

believe I have to go to work."

"It was a total success," she said.

"It was a good party," he said. "I love to give parties. We're very good at it. It's one of the things we do well."

"People liked your play."

"I'm glad, I'm sure. But really, it's kind of pathetic, isn't it, doing it in the living room? It isn't supposed to be a hobby. I'm supposed to be a real playwright."

"You are a real playwright."

"You think that, and I'd like to think that, but the evidence is otherwise. I'm glad we did it. I like the play, I think it's funny, and God knows it's true. I wish I had made them learn the lines. It would have been a lot better. It is hard to believe what you are watching is real when the actors are looking at their scripts all the time. Oh well."

"You should send it out."

"I've despaired of that. Nobody is going to do my plays for me. I have to be there. I have to put my body on the line. Nobody gets them from reading them. If anybody else did it they would screw it up. I've been there. It's agony. Forget it. I don't want to think about it." He went to her and put his arms around her and kissed her. "Thank you for the beautiful backdrop. Thank you for helping so much with everything."

"You're welcome. You help me. Will you bring me another harpsichord? I had a call from Bruno.

"Maybe I can come home for lunch."

"That would be nice."

So he did, and they had siesta while Sam was taking a nap. It was a happy time.

•

Doreen took up belly dancing, going off for lessons one night a week and practicing in the dining room when she was home alone. That's not my kind of music—I am not an Arabian cat, or Turkish, or any of those exotic types—but she liked having an audience, and I was willing to watch. She put me in a chair and directed her wiggling at me, fixing me with her look, whirling, swishing her veils, clinking her finger cymbals. Alicia and Jill came over to rehearse with her, and then they had a party and danced for their husbands, with scarves over the lamps to make the light rosy.

The evening was so much fun that they decided to have an Art Club, with themselves as the members, and meet once a month. David was a writer but the other five were painters. At the first official meeting they closed the curtains, turned up the heat, and took turns posing naked for each other. Jill posed first, taking all her clothes off and standing with one foot up on a stool and an arm raised. They all busily started drawing, even David, and drew for some minutes. David had put on a recording of Chopin.

Jill was quivering slightly. "Are you cold?" Alicia asked. "You're not embarrassed, surely? Maybe this will help." She put down her chalk and took her shirt off. "That's better."

"Any excuse," Stefan said.

"Don't move," Victor said.

"That's not it," Jill said, "I can't hold this pose."

"Just another minute," Stefan said. The two men were furiously busy scribbling on their drawing pads, looking at her fiercely, then at the paper, like it was a race.

"Breathe," Victor said, his crayon dancing on the page. "Your arm is attached to a balloon. The balloon is holding it up. It is floating. It weighs *nothing.*"

"My leg," she said, starting to collapse, collapsing.

"That was so beautiful," Victor said.

"Yeow," she said, rubbing her calf. "I'm getting

a cramp. Sorry. Can I sit down? I don't want to stop."

Joey was on the stairs, quietly looking on through the balustrade. Noticing him, Doreen said, "Go to bed, Joey."

"Any position is fine," Stefan said. "Sit on the stool. Be comfortable."

"We're having an art class," David explained. "A life class. I'll come up with you. I can't do this anyway." He looked at his drawing with distaste. "I'll be back." He disappeared upstairs with Joey while the others drew another picture of Jill. I reclined on the window seat, drifting in and out. Why weren't they drawing me?

David came back down. "Let me pose now so Jill can draw," he said, taking off his clothes. "I love to get naked." Jill put her clothes on.

Alicia had already put her shirt back on. "It's more interesting if only one person is exposed," she said. "I'll go next."

Doreen asked, "Are they asleep?"

"They're fine. He's not traumatized, don't worry. We really are artists. It's perfectly legitimate."

"Of course it is," said Stefan, "but this is not Paris. Small-town America is not necessarily as broad-minded as thee and me."

"He won't say anything. He doesn't think anything of it. We're always like this." David sprawled back in an easy chair, throwing a leg over the arm. "What do you think? Can everybody see everything?"

They all busily started drawing.

•

They invited Lewis Cotter to dinner so David could talk to him about starting a theatre at the church down the street and it turned into rather a strange scene, which I watched with a certain foreboding. Lewis was a tall, suave young man, closer to Doreen's age than David's.

She was suspicious of David's interest in him.

"You may be right, but I don't think so," he said. "Anyway he's straight. I don't want to have sex with him, I want to start a theatre with him. Doing art together would be more satisfying than having an affair. I don't want anyone but you."

"You're kidding yourself but you're not fooling me."

"I need his energy. I can't do anything by myself. You're right that I don't believe it's real. But that's the way things start, the vaguest idea in someone's head that seems like nothing until other people buy into it, and pretty soon you have a large building with dozens of people doing what they love. I know it's just a fantasy, but if I could get Lewis involved it would happen." Lewis's father owned the newspaper.

"Well good luck," she said. "What do you want to have for dinner?"

"I'll make a curry."

"I'll make a pie."

"That would be lovely."

The night he came there were some strange vibrations around the table after the boys went up to their room. Was she right about David's real motive? Lewis was blandly positive about the theatre, but that part of the conversation never came into focus. Meanwhile he had been pressing Doreen's foot under the table and now his hand was creeping up her leg. David saw it, and they saw he saw it. David said, "I'd really like to work with you so I hope you will give it some serious consideration and we can make it happen." He got up and started clearing the table. When he was out of the room Lewis leaned over and whispered something in Doreen's ear. Not long after that he took his leave.

"What was that?" David said later in the

kitchen. "I thought I was the one who was supposed to be trying to seduce him. What are you doing?"

"Nothing. None of your business."

"Well don't be hostile all of a sudden. I didn't do anything."

"Neither did I."

"I know, but what are you thinking?"

"I'm not thinking anything. I'm thinking how much I want to go to bed and go to sleep."

"I'll wash the dishes."

"You're an angel, sometimes."

"Give me a kiss." She went over to him and leaned in and kissed him, and he pulled her close, but she pulled away and picking up a book from the shelf went up the back stairs.

That was not the end of it. I knew nothing and didn't want to know anything. Why couldn't they just chill? Life was good. But something was eating at one or both of them.

They went on a picnic on a Saturday and came back smelling of cow pasture. "Why are you punishing me?" she said out of the blue as they were putting things away.

"I'm not punishing you. Should I be? Have you done something bad?"

"Don't talk to me like that."

"Of course, you don't believe in psychology. You don't admit the existence of the unconscious."

"I don't know what you're talking about."

"That's what I mean."

"I'm not stupid."

"I know you're not, but you act stupid, not wanting to listen to any slightly complicated idea or understand anything the least bit subtle. Come on!"

"I'll see you later," she said. She walked through the house and out the front door. David came out on the front porch and we watched her walk away up the sidewalk and out of sight.

"Don't you want to know where I was?" she said when she came back.

"Where were you?"

"At Lewis's."

"Really!" He seemed surprised. "I couldn't imagine where you had gone. What was that like?"

"It was O.K."

"Are you still mad? I'm sorry I attacked you. I don't know what got into me. Did you sleep with him?"

"If you want to call it that."

"Was this the first time?"

"No."

"Ah. Well. Are you happy?"

"I'm going to bed," she said, her characteristic way of ending a conversation.

"I think Charles and I will stay up for a while and play music." She kissed him good night and went up. As a Christmas present Rolf had made a special bench for David's harpsichord that was wide enough for me to sit beside him while he played. Sometimes he played for an hour or more, played and played, and we lost and found ourselves in the patterns of vibration. It was one of our best ways of being close. I knew what he was doing. I was right there.

Chapter 10

The next fall we had a teenage boy living with us who had come from Holland for a year of high school. David gave him the back bedroom and moved his study up to the attic. Hansi was an only child and liked having Joey and Sam as little brothers. The three boys cleaned out the playhouse in the backyard, which was rotting but usable, and hung out there after school with some other kids from the neighborhood.

"We should talk about Thanksgiving," David said one day when he and Doreen were alone in the basement folding laundry. I didn't usually go down there, in spite of the mouse potential—too many spiders, too damp and musty around the edges.

"Do you have something in mind?"

"Well, what do you want to do? We can go to Rolf and Beth's."

"No, I couldn't stand it. I want to have it here. Let's make a feast. I'll do the turkey if you'll help."

"Of course I will. Oh I'm glad!" he said. "It's really a Thanksgiving kind of house. I love having parties with you."

"Do you want to invite your sister?"

"She wants to come, and Cousin Maude is somewhere around here, I think."

"Living?"

"No no, she still lives in San Francisco. Do you want to invite Lewis?"

"No. He has a girlfriend."

"Since when?"

"Since your play, actually. She came to see her brother in it. That's how they met."

"We can have them both."

"I don't think so."

"Are you all right? You've been looking rather sad."

"It was already over. Forget it."

"I'd like to bring a couple of people from work. You haven't met them. Paul is German and Régine is from Paris. They've never had an American Thanksgiving."

"Do they speak English?"

"His is good," David said, "but hers is rudimentary, and my French is pitiful. I know quite a bit of French vocabulary, I took it for three years, but I am completely unable to speak it. And I never can understand what people are saying. They talk too fast and run all the words together. I can't even understand what they are talking *about.* I am supposed to be teaching Régine about piano actions. She works for Jean-Louis in Paris. So I show her things and explain what she's doing wrong with a lot of lame gestures, and she tries to speak English. It's ridiculous. She seems like an interesting person, though. Paul is something of a thug."

"I want to invite Muriel, my friend who was ditched by her husband and has the kid. She's having a really hard time. I think they're living out of her car. She calls me from pay phones every few days."

"She doesn't sound like very much fun."

"It would be a kindness."

"Definitely invite her. By all means. I hope she comes. We are lucky we have so much to share. I am truly thankful."

•

David and I spent a quiet hour in his study early on Thanksgiving morning, but after that it was accelerating busyness all day preparing for the party. There were numerous people, abundant food and drink, and much animated talk and switching around, too much to take in. I went my own way and nobody bothered me. They would all go away and I would still be here.

The house was full that night, David's sister Bitsy in the front room in the attic, her son Billy in with his cousins on a pallet on the floor. They were planning to go to the cabin for the weekend, leaving me with Rolf and Beth. David had explained it and apologized. It was O.K., they are fun people, I was interested in the baby, and he was right that I didn't want to ride all the way up there in my awful box, cool as it is when you arrive. In the event Doreen decided not to go so I could stay home. She took David out into the yard and talked to him about it while the others were having breakfast.

"Why don't you want to come?"

"You don't want me to," she said. "Bitsy doesn't like me. You'll have more fun if I'm not there."

"I suppose that means *you* don't like *her.* I don't see why not. She likes you well enough. It doesn't matter. *I* want you to come."

"Billy is horribly spoiled. It's all some kind of sick competition."

"It's too easy to have attitudes about the way other people bring up their children. Please come. I really wish you would."

"I'm not coming. I have other plans. Don't worry about it."

"I'm not worried, I just thought we could all be together. Are you depressed? I know, I know it's hard."

Whirly and Sam were both trying to play with me, which was hopelessly distracting. I had to get away from them and didn't hear any more.

•

Once they had all driven away, Doreen made a phone call, and a little later the French woman, Régine, appeared at the front door. Doreen made a point of introducing us. "This is Charles," she said. "Charles, this is Régine." She seemed like a serious person. I had barely noticed her at the Thanksgiving party, except I noticed Doreen was talking to her a lot, or trying to talk to her. They were both weirdly inarticulate. What does it mean to be "French"?

Doreen made tea and they sat at the kitchen table talking more and more quietly until they were almost whispering, leaning close, ignoring me. I had other things to do anyway. Later when it was getting dark I noticed that nobody was turning the lights on. They were up in the bedroom with the door closed. I don't know why they closed the door. Nobody was there except me. Maybe they were cold. Whirly was in the room with them. I didn't care but it did seem a little rude.

Later they left the door ajar so I could go in. Régine stayed all night, went away for a while after breakfast, and came back in the afternoon. She petted me in an interesting way when I sat beside her on the sofa, pressing me against her body. When the phone rang, Doreen let the answering machine pick up. "I'm not here," she said when Régine raised an eyebrow. "Pas ici." They were quiet but oddly excited, eyes glittering. I wondered what was going on. Not that I ever really know, with humans.

David and the boys came back smelling of fresh air. Doreen and Régine had made them a Moroccan dinner, which was lively and festive. The boys told about playing a wild game of capture the flag as it was getting dark. Billy was running away not looking where he was going and went over the edge of the rock and was lucky not to break his neck. Régine listened closely, smiling, but didn't say a single word. After dinner she helped clear the table and dried the dishes as David washed them. She said she had to go and politely thanked David, who walked her to the door and said, "I'll see you tomorrow.

145

Back to work." She left and he flopped down on the living room sofa.

"I'll put the boys to bed," Doreen said.

"That would be nice," he said. Joey and Sam jumped on top of him and he hugged and kissed them.

"I'll come back down," she said from the doorway. "I want to talk to you."

"I want to talk to you too. We missed you."

"I hope not," she said.

"Not too much. We had a good time. It was extremely beautiful. The leaves are down, but there is still color underfoot, and the light comes through the trees in a different way. This is one of my favorite times of year, although the days are getting awfully short."

She and the boys went upstairs. He stretched out on the sofa on his back. I composed myself on his chest and purred. He put his hand on my head and we just lay there. He didn't seem to have to do anything for a change.

We may have fallen asleep. I didn't notice Doreen come in until she was sitting on the coffee table inches away.

David opened his eyes. "What's up?"

"You seem pretty calm."

"I love it there," he said. "It stays with me. Did you have a good weekend? What did you do?"

"I was with Régine."

"Ah. Was that nice? Could you talk?"

"She is learning English and I am learning French."

"That's a good idea. I wish my French was better."

"Why don't you do something about it?"

"Maybe I will. I have started translating a play she gave me by Marguerite Duras. Writing it out seems like a good way of reading it. Otherwise I'm not sure whether I'm getting it or not, I can just skim along and kid myself."

"Don't you want to know what we did?"

"What? Are you having another affair? I thought you were straight."

"Don't be vulgar."

"Sorry, I didn't realize I was."

"She is a very interesting person."

"I know she is. I told you she was. A little strange, though, don't you think? So mysterious about her life. Do you know what happened?"

"What do you mean?"

"She seems to have had some kind of traumatic relationship that's made her live like a nun for the past ten years, something like that, although that may not be the whole story."

"I can't believe you're gossiping about her like this."

"Come on, it's you. It's you and me. It's not gossip, it's privileged communication. Did you actually sleep together?'

"Yes, we slept, we slept. We are becoming intimate friends."

"Well that was fast."

"I can't talk to you."

"You're doing pretty well, it seems to me. Really, I am surprised. You were very definite about not being attracted to other women. What was that? Am I missing something? Is it new? Is it a revelation of your true nature?"

"I'm going over there."

"Don't go. Please."

"I'll see you later."

"How much later? What does that mean?"

"In the morning. I'll try to be here before the boys get up."

"I don't think this is going to work," he said. "I am very understanding, but she had you all weekend, and I just got back. I don't think it's quite fair, do you?"

"She is leaving in a few days. She is going back to Paris. I need to talk to her."

"Call her on the phone. Oh forget it. Go ahead. I don't want you if you don't want to be here."

I couldn't think what to do so the next day I pissed in the sofa, in the back of the seat behind the cushions. Nobody noticed. They had found the sofa on the street, and it was very nice. The boys had a new trick, taking turns standing on the arm and then falling over backwards into the soft down cushions. It was just barely long enough for Joey; soon he'd be hitting his head. Doreen didn't think they should do it but David said it was O.K. With that going on, nobody was really sitting there. So I did it again the next day, and the day after that, until Doreen noticed the smell and told David when he came home from work. "He's your cat," she said. He was unusually firm with me, pushing my face down into the crack and speaking to me severely. Doreen left before dinner and didn't come back until it was time for him to go work in the morning so I did it again. Again she told David about it when he came home. This time he went berserk, chasing me around the house with a broom, screaming at me, completely out of his mind. Joey and Sam got into the act and tried to corner me. Hansi stuck his head out of his room but luckily for me decided not to intervene. It was wild. We hadn't had so much excitement in a long time. I don't remember ever, actually.

"David, stop," Doreen said the second or third time we went past. "He gets it. You're just playing with him now."

"I am not playing with him," he said, panting. "I am trying to frighten him. I want him to think I will kill him if he does it again."

Good heavens! What a goof I am! It was her I was trying to get at, and here I had driven him right over the brink. I was glad to see him put away the broom. I was crouched on the stairs halfway up, looking through the banister.

"Well, that was exciting," he said, coming back into the living room. He started to sit on the sofa, thought better of it, and sat on the window seat instead. "Are you O.K.?"

"I'm just sad."

"I'm not. I like her very much, but you knew she was going back. She's French. And you're married to me."

"Am I still?"

"Certainly. Please come back. I need you. We

all do."

"Oh David," she said, kneeling at his feet and laying her head in his lap. He patted her on the shoulder and stroked her head, which I can testify he is very good at. She cried a little, and he said, "There, there." It was very sweet. I couldn't take credit for it, I suppose, but I was gratified to say the least, especially when they went around turning the lights off and climbed the stairs hand in hand and went off to bed in the love mood. What a relief!

I was sorry about the sofa, but I had to do something.

•

They brought home several fish, which lived in a bubbling tank on a shelf in the back hall, little bitty fish that floated aimlessly around in the glowing tank and occasionally died. They were afraid I would eat the fish and made a big deal about keeping the top on the tank, but I couldn't jump that high, for one thing, and I was nowhere near as interested in the fish as I was in Caruso, the canary they kept in a cage in their bedroom. His cage was well out of reach on a tall stand, but they sometimes took it down to clean it and change the paper, and I watched closely as they opened the door and reached in, the bright little bird fluttering wildly at the top of the cage. There was a complicated latch that I probably couldn't work even if I could reach it. But Caruso wanted out as much as I wanted in so I kept an eye on him. You never know.

Doreen decorated a series of harpsichords for Bruno. David began going to concerts and writing reviews for the newspaper, often taking Joey or Sam with him, coming home late and carrying the boy into the house sound asleep. Sam was going to playschool some mornings, and Hansi was pursuing high school, excited about acting in a play. David had acquired a baby grand piano and played for Hansi to practice his songs.

It was just starting to be spring when Doreen went to Paris to look at antique harpsichords and visit Régine. Sam had to go to a different play school where he could stay later but otherwise her absence didn't make much of a difference. Hansi was there to baby-sit when needed, and David liked cooking. She was back before anyone missed her too much and said she got a lot out of it. By then there were a couple of hours of daylight after David got home from work, and he helped her till a vegetable garden and planted flowers while the boys kicked a soccer ball around.

•

Hansi left at the end of the school year, his English much improved. The yard was beautiful, and David fired up the barbecue for a big picnic on the Fourth of July, with everybody we knew in attendance, including the Ludwigs' pooch, Serena, who was refined and good-mannered if a bit thick. I took her out to show her the berry patch in the neighbors' yard, much favored by moles and gophers, which she seemed to like in her ditsy way.

Régine came back in August to work for Bruno for another month and slept in the front room in the attic. I didn't try to keep track of where Doreen slept but I saw her going back and forth. Régine rode in to work with David every morning and worked with him on a literary project in his study in the other half of the attic whenever they had a chance, poring over a text and discussing the exact wording in fanatical detail. He argued for a certain spontaneity, but she had very strong feelings about which words he was allowed to use.

David took Joey and Sam up to the cabin the first weekend Régine was there. I made him understand I wanted to go too. He had a station wagon now, and with my box up higher so I could see more, the trip was not bad at all. We had a wonderful time in the country. They made a fire outside and cooked over it. As darkness came on David led us along a path through the woods to the top of an enormous sloping meadow where they lay on their backs in the grass and watched the stars come out. There were mice in the field but I didn't feel like chasing them. I didn't see any other significant animals. David made me sleep inside so the coyotes wouldn't eat me. But there was no sign of coyotes.

We came home relaxed and happy, if a bit frazzled from the road. Régine had made dinner and served it family style at the big table in the dining room.

"Are you going to sleep with me?" David asked Doreen when they were alone in their bedroom getting ready for bed.

"We could all three sleep together," Doreen proposed in reply. "She likes you."

"I like her," he said, "but I don't really think that's a good idea. Three-way sex has a certain charm as a novelty, perhaps, but it doesn't really work."

"We don't have to do anything."

"I know. But we would."

"I'd like it."

"I'd like it too. I always like sex," he said, "but it's way too complicated. I don't think you could handle it, frankly. It would get too emotional and weird. I only want to sleep with you."

"I'm going to go ask her."

"Whatever. It turns me on, actually, the mere idea." I could see that David was getting into that funny state that seems to take him over and make him want to touch his penis and rub it against people or objects or just rub it. Naked in the bed, he was not really doing this now but I could tell he was thinking about it.

After Doreen went upstairs he uncovered his penis and looked at it, squeezing it in his hand, then put it away and picked up a book. He was absorbed in reading when she rather sheepishly reappeared.

"Well?"

"She was shocked."

"Really."

"She was embarrassed."

"That isn't the way to do it," he said. "It has to arise naturally."

"I'm so embarrassed."

"Come to bed."

She took off her wrap and climbed into bed. He turned off the light. A full moon was shining in the windows.

"I don't want her to feel bad," she said.

"She's a big girl."

" She's very sensitive and vulnerable."

"Don't get defensive. I am nothing but friendly to her. I need her help. And I like her."

"I'm going up."

"Oh please!"

"It's all right. She's just here for a little while."

She got up and went. David turned on the radio beside the bed and we lay listening to music in the silky dark.

Such peace was not to be. Doreen reappeared a few minutes later obviously upset.

"What's the matter?"

"Can I sleep with you?"

"Of course. I wish you would. Don't you know that?"

She got in bed and lay rather stiffly on her side.

"She won't let me touch her. She says it would be unfair to you. Do you think that's true?"

"I think you are perhaps being a little greedy, but that's all right, greedy for love. You have a true heart."

"I do."

"If you didn't, you wouldn't know it. I want to believe that sanity will prevail. Régine is quite sane, I think. She is certainly smart. We are having a wonderful time working on the play."

"I'm so unhappy."

"Are you? That's too bad. You should be happy. Everybody loves you."

"Really?"

"You can touch *me*," he said. "Here, let me put my arms around you. Relax, my love. Everything's fine. You can have your cake and eat it too. But don't forget to keep a piece for me."

"Are you all right?"

"Thank you for asking. I'm fine. I so much love being a daddy. I love this life and my little family. This is the most precious time. It's nice having Régine here. I'm fine. You'll be all right. Don't worry. You can have everything."

They kissed; I heard the little lip noises and sighs. Then gradually instead of quieting down they started moving around rather vigorously under the covers. Finally David rudely pushed me right off the bed. I went to the door and scratched, which he hates, and he got up and let me out.

Chapter 11

We tried to get along and it should have been perfectly easy; instead waves of desperation kept breaking over us, often in sync with lunar cycles but nonetheless real. The boys were lively and demanding, and everybody had routines that swept them along. David and Doreen should have been happy, both pursuing personal projects in addition to their paying work, writing, making books, painting, though never enough to satisfy themselves, apparently. Much of the time they were barely speaking to one another, chillier and chillier as the chilly season wore on. It rubbed off on the boys, too, Joey unnecessarily mean to Sam, Sam deliberately provoking him. David wouldn't let them fight, insisting on harmony; Doreen got into it with them when he wasn't there. Caruso sang along with Maria Callas. Whirly and I were cool. But the fish had all died.

When it was good it was very good. They had a tremendous Christmas party bringing together many large and small humans, who all had a wonderful time. David played his new piano and people sang. Doreen produced all kinds of good food. For New Year's David cooked a duck just for the two of them. After the boys were asleep, they ate at a little table by candlelight and drank champagne. It was really perfect.

Mostly the winter was miserable, and they kept getting sick. With Doreen it was often not clear whether she was unhappy or unwell or both, but she struggled on. It emerged eventually that she had an infection requiring doctor visits and medicines, and for a while they couldn't do anything in bed to cheer themselves up even if they wanted to.

When David got sick it was sudden and total; he took to his bed, gave in completely to being taken care of by Doreen and the two boys, did nothing but write in his notebook and listen to music on the radio. I spent the whole day with him, lounging around on the foot of the bed. I loved it. Then he got up and went back to work.

•

Needing money to go to Paris again, Doreen tried to get Bruno to pay her more for decorating his harpsichords. He counterattacked and made her cry, and she quit or was fired.

"I'm going to Paris anyway," she said a few weeks later.

"What do you mean, anyway?"

"You don't want me to go. You want me to stay here and cook and clean and look after your children. Our children."

"I can cook, although I am pretty exhausted when I get home from work. We're trying to get caught up while Bruno is in California. When he gets back he'll throw a wrench in the works and we'll be back where we started. I don't mind housework. Marlene Dietrich said it was her favorite activity, although she was probably fibbing. And I love to be with the boys, whenever I am not working. When are you thinking of going?"

"In April, for a month."

"I don't mind you going, but a month is too long. Go for two weeks. We can handle that."

"I'm going for a month."

"Or three weeks. Three weeks at the most. I thought a month would be O.K. the first time but it's not. After three weeks it's not like you're on a trip, it's like you're gone, we're on our own, we have to get used to it, and it's hard to get back to where we were."

"I need more time."

"What for? You're not painting harpsichords anymore. You can't pretend it's research. How are you going to pay for it?"

"I still have some money. It's only the airfare. Régine will take care of me while I'm there."

"I can't believe you've been holding money back to spend on yourself like this. Can't you help me support the family a little bit? I'm working three jobs. I don't keep any of it for myself. When was the last time I had a personal jaunt, apart from a few days at the cabin once in a blue moon? Jesus Christ!"

"Don't work yourself up."

"All right, I'll be cool. I will. But it's very hard on the boys. They don't know what to think. Are you leaving me?"

"No, I'm just going to Paris. I wish you could go too."

"Let's move to France," he said.

"That's a good idea."

"I'm sick of working for Bruno. He's never going to change. He's a genius and he's impossible. It's unbearable. But what would I do? I can't even talk to people. I'm stuck here."

"Well I'm not."

"A short trip is fine," he said. "I don't want to bring you down. Just don't stay away so long."

Joey wept dramatically and Sam acted cool

when their mommy said goodbye. At first her absence was an improvement, she had been so moody. Undistracted, David gave his sons extra attention and thought of fun things to do with them. Doreen had arranged for a babysitter to meet the boys after school and stay with them until David got home from work. He took them up to the cabin one weekend, leaving me alone in the house with Caruso, who got on my nerves singing behind the closed bedroom door, like a wind-up bird that never runs down. I spent ten days with the Schmidts while David took the boys to California to see their grandparents, which would have been a nice change except that Gretchen, their little girl, was at a very annoying age, "cute," everybody agreed, but relentless, chasing me around the house, babbling, "Kitty kitty kitty," insisting on holding me in her arms or laying me across her lap. There was something obscene about it. I am not a kitty; I never was. I may be fixed but I am still male, and certainly grown up. So I was glad to go home.

David went to work, and the machinery started rolling again, but then it immediately broke down. Sam had fits of screaming in the night, neither awake nor asleep, apparently terrified. David held him and carried him around, reassuring him, singing to him, but it had no effect; eventually he quieted down and slept the rest of the night, remembering nothing in the morning. Joey was more nervous than usual.

The babysitter flaked out, leaving Sam stranded at school; David left work early to pick him up. The babysitter came back for a day, then quit altogether. Joey could walk over from his school to Sam's and pick him up and walk him home through the park, he was old enough, and they could let themselves in and have a snack and be all right for a couple of hours. That worked for a few days, but then Joey got sick, throwing up in the middle of the night and unwilling to go to school the next day. David was prepared to stay home, but Joey felt better once the school bus had come and gone, and David took him to work with him. Then Sam came down with chicken pox, which was more serious and lasted for days. David called Doreen in Paris and begged her to come home; instead she extended her trip for another week. He eventually found another babysitter and everybody survived, but a little dazed from their various ordeals.

Doreen came back with a different energy,

purposive and distant.

"How was it this time?" David asked. "How is Régine? You didn't send a single postcard."

"I made you a painting of George Sand."

"I love it," he said.

"Can you leave me the car?"

"Sure. It's better to carpool anyway. It's silly to all drive separate cars, and it gets me out of there on time."

She waited until he was gone and then drove off and stayed away all day.

"I called you this afternoon, but you weren't here," he said one night. "You're never here. Where are you going all the time? Do you have a secret life?"

"It's no secret," she said. "I met some very interesting women in New London who have a shop, and they want me to paint on silk for them."

"Are you working there?"

"I am painting, but I am not working. But I will be, maybe. It could be quite lucrative."

"We're barely getting by," he said. "If my father hadn't paid for the heating oil I don't know what we would have done."

"I'm going to make a lot of money one of these days so you can quit your job and just write and direct plays. It makes me sick to see you wasting your time working for Bruno."

"That would be wonderful. I hope you do."

"I will. I really feel it. I'm good at this."

"Another new medium."

"The colors are a revelation, transparent and glowing. I am working with a designer who has amazing ideas."

"These women, are they…?"

"What?"

"Oh never mind."

"Lesbians? Yes they are. They are strong women. I can't tell you how much better it feels to work with women instead of being pushed around by men all the time."

"Do I push you around?"

"I don't mean you. I mean Bruno."

"I know you mean Bruno. He pushes me around too. I know what you mean."

"You're not a woman."

"Well, no, sorry. I think you *do* mean me, if you don't mind my saying so. I don't know what to do about it. It's ironic, isn't it. Are they paying you anything?"

"Not yet."

•

166

The doorbell rang on a Saturday around noon. It was the landlord, whose wife had inherited the house, announcing that we would have to move: they were giving the house to their daughter as a wedding present. This set in motion the most radical rearrangement of our lives yet.

David and Doreen were stunned and pretended nothing had happened. It was a few days before I heard them say anything about it. I thought maybe I had imagined it.

"Did you find any houses to look at yet?" David asked at dinner.

"No, I was too busy, and then when I came home I was too tired."

"You can find us another house," David said. "You've done it before. I have complete confidence in you."

"You can do it, Mommy," Joey said.

"We'll never find another house as nice as this one," she said.

"That's probably true, but you never know. Maybe we should move out into the country. I'd like that," he said. "How do you think it would be for the boys?"

"I don't want to move," Sam said.

"Neither do I," David said. "I wish we didn't

have to."

But she didn't do anything about it, and neither did he, and the clock was ticking. The school year ended. The long evenings were sweet, flowers they had planted blooming all around the house, which had never looked better. Doreen had not planted a vegetable garden because they would not be there for the harvest.

David went away for some days on harpsichord business. While he was gone she did a lot of phoning, and when he came back, she told him she was leaving, taking the boys and moving to New Mexico.

"What? Why? How could you do that? I know, it's terrible about the house, but we'll be all right."

"I am a battered wife," she said.

"What are you talking about? I never hit you. I wouldn't."

"You hit me in the kitchen in Stonington. You pushed me down."

"That was years ago. It was once. I was sick about it. You forgave me."

"You're pitiful. You're short on the milk of human kindness. You'll be sorry."

"I *am* sorry. I am sorry all the time."

"Just wait till you have another spouse and

you will realize how patient I have been with you."

"Is this what love is?"

"I can't talk to you."

"What about Régine? What does she say?"

"It has nothing to do with Régine."

"Is there someone else?"

"I am saving my *life*," she said. "This isn't easy for me."

"Go," he said, "you already broke my heart several times, it is broken, I don't care anymore. But you can't take Joey and Sam away."

"You can't deal with them."

"Well, I just did. It wasn't easy, but we made it."

"What would they do all day while you're at work? I can't leave them. It would kill me."

"I know how unhappy you have been. I've tried as hard as I can to make you happy. I thought you were happy. Maybe this will be better for you and me, I don't know, but I feel terrible for the boys. I am in a state of acute discontent myself. I saw this coming. You have been threatening to leave for years. I did everything I could to save our marriage, and so did you, but the truth is, we both want something else. I'm not a factory worker. I hate working for Bruno. He makes himself big by belittling everybody around him."

"I've been telling you that all along."

"I'm a writer, but I have a family to support, and somehow I got trapped."

"Well, now you're free."

"I don't want to lose my children."

"You won't. You can see them as much as you want. I don't want to take them away from you, but you can't deal with them by yourself, and I don't want to lose them either."

"Why are you doing this? Can't we just be happy?"

"No. It's not enough to pretend. Can't you be honest for a change?"

"I'm trying," he said.

"Well, try harder."

She filled up the enclosed front porch with furniture and boxes to be shipped to her in New Mexico. Her father would pay for the movers. The house was coming apart. Joey was frantic. Sam was calm, as if nothing out of the ordinary was going on, but he had night frights a couple of times that showed how he was really feeling.

And then the day came and they left. David drove them to the airport in Boston so I was spared the farewell scene. Whirly was traveling in my box. I imagined Joey wailing and clinging to his Daddy, Sam unflappable, Doreen fiercely determined, David grimly good-natured. I had never seen him as miserable as he was when he came home alone.

A truck came and took away Doreen's stuff. The house looked better with less clutter, the sun gleaming on the floors in the empty rooms. Caruso went on singing, and David and I were closer than ever. Is this what is meant by a mixed blessing?

•

I had the impression that everything would change after that, but David went right on going to work every day, and instead of moving to New York, we only moved a few blocks. Victor and Jill were transplanting themselves to Maine and arranged for David to take over their apartment upstairs from an antique shop in an older part of town. Victor had completely refurbished it so David didn't have to do anything. Their studio was next door, a big second-story loft, and he tried to rent that too, imagining a theatre, but the landlord demurred and he let it go. Rolf, Stefan, and a couple of friends from work pitched in to help him move, and there we were.

It was definitely a come-down from the last couple of houses we had lived in, but not too bad. Caruso was installed in the bedroom, my litter box in the bathroom behind the tub, and David set my bowls in the kitchen beside the stove. There were more small rooms up a narrow flight of stairs, but he didn't have any use for them. The special feature was a large porch on the back of the house, enclosed on three sides and perfectly private. He could eat outside even if it was raining.

There was a cat door, for a change, and I made the most of it, going out whenever I felt the urge, down the outside stairs and nosing through the strange collection of old buildings in the center of the block, most of them empty and unused. I had no trouble getting in and out of them, but I came home quite dirty, which made David wonder what I was up to; fortunately he was never a worrier. I expected other cats, but no one was there. I was the king.

•

What was the meaning of my life? I couldn't help wondering. I mean, I don't care where I live. Inside, outside, mansion, shack, I can find a cozy spot and make myself comfortable. I like making new maps of territory in my mind and practicing and testing myself. And if I don't have to, fine. I don't have to do anything. I am satisfied to lie around, nap, go for a stroll now and then, stretch, roll over, wash, eat, you know, the usual. I don't need anything else. Please don't imagine I am a typical cat. Many of my kind pursue their lives in a state of cringing paranoia; others live only for food, or crave attention from their people, always demanding, begging, rubbing up against their legs. Thank heavens my younger years were trauma-free, apart from that hideous run-in in California. I see too many warped personalities. I had become a connoisseur of being, not afraid to be perfectly contented.

At this point, however, my confidence in my person, always crucial to my well-being, was sorely shaken. Think about it. My entire life till now had been defined by David and Doreen; outward circumstances changed, but they were what it was about, essentially. I was formed to their ways. I was his cat, of course, but she was an animal person and continuously aware of me. He was more of a floating spirit, mellow and generally benevolent but capable of dangerous explosions and lapses of flakiness. He was my one, definitely, and vice versa, but we had always been part of a larger system overseen by her and actively branching—Joey, Sam, other animals. Whoosh, they were all gone, and it was just me and him, oddly static and at the same time unstable, needing a third leg. Regrettably neither of us could really understand Caruso's language (Italian?), not that I wanted to talk to him.

So what about my confidence in myself? I had been part of the glue that held them together. I had failed. What good was I?

It was hard to know what David was thinking, now that there was no one there for him to chew things over with. Luckily for me, though, he talked on the "telephone" more than ever, holding it to his ear and talking into it as if there was a tiny person inside, and there was: you could hear the person's tiny voice. That helped me make sense of his comings and goings—not that I needed to, as long as he came home every night to feed me and mucked out my box. I could drink out of the toilet, which he never neglected to flush.

He had long, intense conversations with Rolf and other people about anxious goings-on at the harpsichord factory. Apparently Bruno was losing his grip. They talked about staging a takeover, but it fizzled, as had the idea of starting a theatre with Lewis. David half-hoped the business would go under and he would be liberated; he was too "shook up," he said, to think about doing anything else. Several times he talked to Doreen, his voice shaking with emotion, about coming out to join her in New Mexico, saying he missed the boys terribly, he would be able to find something to do, they would be happy again, but she discouraged him. He got very low but then cheered up the next time they talked: Bruno was talking about sending him to Paris to work for a while. Paris? What about me?

I almost got Caruso. One day David took down his cage and set it on the bedroom floor on layers of newspapers to give it a thorough cleaning. He opened the door and reached in and started pulling things out. When he turned away for a moment, Caruso inquisitively hopped up onto the edge of the door frame and then hopped out. I was under the bed, ready, and I was on him in a flash. I actually had a paw on him, loosing a tiny puff of yellow fluff, before David grabbed the bird and knocked me away. To have touched his bony little body was a lingering thrill; I could feel it in my paw for days.

•

Joey came for Christmas, which brightened our lives for a couple of weeks. Another daddy with two boys who were friends of Joey's came for Christmas dinner. They all worked on talking David into getting a computer and a tv to be a monitor for it. David hated tv, they had never had one, but he admitted he wanted to watch tennis. After dinner they played balloon badminton in the living room. I tried to get into the game and accidentally popped the balloon.

Joey went back to Doreen after New Year's, although Doreen, I gathered, was going off to Paris again and leaving the boys with her sister Susie, which made David crazy. He tried to talk her out of going, talked about keeping Joey, bringing Sam back to live with him, going to New Mexico to be with them while she was away, but nothing changed.

That winter he was writing almost all the time he was home. After Christmas he directed a play in a nearby town, rushing off to rehearsal every night after a quick dinner, apologizing to me as if I minded what he did, which I did, a little. Then he started going into New York practically every weekend. It felt like I might be losing him, just as he feared losing his sons, but when he was there it was sweeter than ever; I sensed some new mutual sympathy I couldn't quite grasp but enjoyed very much.

Then all of a sudden he did go to Paris, or so he said. I was summarily taken to live with Beth and Rolf. If I had been asked, I don't know what I would have said, but it wasn't bad, actually. Their style was much calmer and more cat-centered than what I was used to, and there was more going on. They had three cats of their own, a big grandma I found strangely attractive, a sassy young mother who regarded me as hopelessly old and wanted nothing to do with me, and an adorable kitten. There were sparks between us at first, but the humans pretty much forced us to get along, which was fine with me. Gretchen, happily, had grown up a bit and was not nearly such a pest.

David had specifically told me he was coming back, but maybe I had misunderstood. Weeks stretched into months. I started to think this was my life. Then he suddenly reappeared one evening and made a big fuss over me. I was not amused and thought about giving him a good nip, to teach him a lesson, but I just stalked off and glared at him from across the room. He knew I was mad.

"Charles looks well," he said as they were sitting down to dinner. "Thank you for taking such good care of him."

"He's just a big baby," Beth said.

"How was Paris?" Rolf asked.

"I loved it. I wish I could live there. But my French is hopeless. It's embarrassing."

"Tell us about it," Beth said.

"Well, where to start. Régine was incredibly good to me. The first day was crazy. I was exhausted from the flight, which was horrible, some cheap French tour airline that didn't even have real seats. She met me at Orly and took me directly to the early music expo at the Grand Palais, where Bruno was holding court in Jean-Louis's booth. The exhibition was fabulous. In the afternoon they took me in a car to look at an old piano, an actual Walther, supposedly, which I was supposed to diagnose and possibly fix up. It was exquisite but completely out of whack. I made a date to come back and work on it. We went back to the Grand Palais for a couple of hours, and then Régine made me walk from there all the way to her apartment near the Luxembourg

Garden, along the Seine, across the Pont Neuf, along the quais and up the Boul' Miche. Paris is so beautiful, it's overwhelming, and there are so many interesting-looking people. I could barely keep going but there was no way to resist her enthusiasm, she loves Paris so much, and so wanted to show it to me. She has a pretty two-room studio on a narrow crooked street, and she gave me some soup. I was starving. I collapsed on her bed and slept for a couple of hours. She woke me up and we went on the Metro to Place d'Itallie, where I was set up to stay with her sister Vivienne. We had dinner with her family, who are all very nice. I had a little room up on the top floor with running water and a squat toilet in the hall. I went down to their apartment to take baths. They invited me to come down for coffee and bread every morning. It was bourgeois, very nice. Jean-Louis's workshop is in a suburb. I took the Metro to Châtelet and changed to the RER. I loved everything about it. I finished two piano actions while I was there. Régine was working in the shop and translated for me when I needed to talk to anyone, but mostly I just worked. I went on a couple of trips to deliver or fix instruments, and I spent two weeks in Provence working on a piano. That was heaven on earth."

"Are she and Doreen still hooking up?"

"I don't think so. I think Doreen has somebody else in the wings, I'm not sure. I practically got it on with Régine myself, we really like each other, but I thought it would be irresponsible so I refrained. Which I regret. I am very lonely."

Gretchen, pajama-clad, climbed on his lap in the living room after dinner. I sat against him on the other side, and everything felt almost normal again. Better, in fact, since he wasn't contending with an unhappy wife or a freshly broken heart. But then the evening came to an end, and he left and didn't take me with him, not saying anything about his intentions this time.

"He doesn't look happy," Beth remarked as Rolf was washing the dishes.

"I don't know," he said.

"Does he still want to get back together with her? I don't see it happening. She doesn't want a man. What was it like with her?"

"Good," he said. "Normal."

"What does that mean? Did she like being fucked, pardon the expression?"

"I guess."

"I'm asking."

"Yes, yes, I thought so. It was her idea. Well, not really, it was my idea, but I wasn't that serious until she bought into it. She was the one who wanted to keep it going."

"Didn't you feel a little manipulated?"

"I didn't mind. And then it worked out."

"It was pretty funny, actually."

"Are you still in love with him?"

"So what if I am? Is it doing any harm? He doesn't mind. We don't have to do anything."

"Shouldn't we tell Gretchen?"

"No, it would only confuse her. You're a wonderful daddy. She doesn't need two."

"Do you?"

"No, of course not. You're all I want."

It was good to be with people who were happy together. I was happy too, or happy enough. My life with David and Doreen gradually faded from memory, its joys and sorrows like a shaggy-dog story someone I used to know had told me long ago. Our apartment was still waiting—Beth kept reminding Rolf to water the plants—but David was away on another trip. I didn't know if he was coming back or not. Better make the best of it.

Chapter 12

Still, I was glad when David came for me and took me away. Beth and Rolf were very nice, I have no complaints, but honestly I prefer being the one cat to being one of several, and there has always been something special about my David. Maybe it's just that I've known him so long, and he me. I wanted to play out our story to the end.

Seriously, something happens between a cat and his person that can't easily be explained. You don't want anything particular from him, you just want him there. David was as wild as I was underneath and we knew that was the best part of us. We had a kind of animal sympathy for each other, if I can put it that way, an instinctive awareness that the comforts of life are precious and fragile and good behavior is a choice. We counted on our good luck to keep us afloat, and if it didn't, well, we would tough it out, live in our bodies as well as we could, and keep looking for grace, which comes more naturally to cats than people, although I know it's rude to say so.

David had Joey and Sam with him now, but not Doreen. It was a pleasure to go back to our no longer lonely apartment. It was summer again, and one of Régine's nephews came from France to keep the boys company while David was at work. I went with them to the cabin for a week, and that was great; they went on other jaunts on other weekends, leaving me on my own. Many days the three kids were stuck in the apartment. It was a good scene; I liked being with them and walking around on them when they sat on the sofa. They played Monopoly, and I walked right across the board, not knocking anything over until Jean-Marc tried to pick me up, and then the little red and green things flew all over. When it was hot they wanted to go to the beach; unfortunately Jean-Marc was too young to drive. So they hung out on the porch, drinking lemonade and making up tricks to do in the hammock. Joey was especially good at wrapping the sides up over his body and spinning around, which made him laugh.

Although we were reasonably joyful, and happy with each other, we had scarcely recovered from Doreen's defection; just below the surface lurked a gloomy vibe that no one could escape for long. Caruso, who had been a kind of symbol of David and Doreen's romance, had boarded at the pet shop while he was away, and I don't know what had happened to him. He was supposed to have a girlfriend there and make babies. Maybe it didn't work out and he was depressed. Whatever the reason, he no longer sang. Maybe it did work out and he no longer needed to sing. He still looked tantalizingly tasty, flipping about on his perch, and I missed his music.

Jean-Marc went back to France; Sam went back to New Mexico; Joey stayed on with his dad. School started. David got up early and typed for an hour, then had breakfast with Joey and got him off to school, then went to work. They were calmer than usual. I was sleeping more than I used to.

I like calm. I don't get bored, but they do, evidently; they always have to be doing things. David was always trying to write. Joey kept on about a computer until David bought one for him from his friends' savvy dad, who hooked it up to a small tv and got Joey started. Working it was too slow and clumsy for David, who stuck to his typewriter, but Joey quickly figured it out and entertained himself playing games on it. Neither of them was interested in watching anything on tv.

The power went out in a big storm, and we

weathered another hurricane in another creaking wooden house.

•

They went into the city to a party and came back with a different energy. "What did you think of all that?" David asked Joey the next night as they were eating spaghetti. "Specifically, what did you think of Marco?"

"He's cool," Joey said.

"I hadn't seen him in five years. He's supposed to be your godfather. I used to visit him whenever I went into the city, but he sent me a postcard five years ago telling me to stay away so he could concentrate on survival. He had a five-year plan. It looks like it worked."

"I don't know what you're talking about."

"Those are my oldest dearest friends. I hadn't seen any of them in years. It's like I'm in exile here. This isn't my real life."

"Is this a dream?"

"No, no. You're real, you and me, definitely. This is real life. I just miss all those interesting people."

"You should go back."

"I can't go back."

"Why not?"

"I have a job. We're here. You're going to school."

"I called that number you brought me, from the library, about Dungeons and Dragons," Joey said one day. "I wish you would play with me."

"I tried," David said. "I just didn't get it. I'm sorry."

"You think it's stupid."

"No, I just think it's weird to have all the real and fantasy medieval stuff scrambled up. How are you supposed to know what reality is when it's all turned into cartoons?"

"You think it's stupid."

"I suppose I do, but it doesn't matter. Tennis is stupid, and I like that."

"I can play with them."

"Who?"

"John. And Joan, and one or two others."

"Do you know anything about them?"

"He asked me how old I am."

"What did you tell him?"

"Ten. I'm ten. He's twenty-two. I said I'm not prejudiced. They'll pick me up."

"When?"

"Saturday morning. Is that O.K.?"

"How long do they play, do you know?"

"All weekend. They'll bring me back."

"You have to do your homework."

"I'll do it Friday night."

"I thought we were going to the movies on Friday night."

"I'll do it Sunday night. You can meet him when he comes to pick me up."

John turned out to have no front teeth, and Joan had black lipstick and fingernails and black lines around her eyes, but otherwise they seemed normal enough. Joey went off with them and didn't come back until Sunday afternoon, saying he'd had pizza, Pepsis, and a good time, the game was great. That became the pattern, weekdays in sync, weekends doing their own thing, and I was starting to relax when David suddenly announced, "I quit my job."

"Good for you," Joey said.

"I had to. Otherwise Bruno would have had to fire me. Business is terrible. The European market has collapsed, and there really wasn't much for me to do. I like working, but I hate jobs where I don't have anything to do. That's the worst."

"What are we going to do now?"

"I'm getting some money from the pension fund so we'll be all right for a few months."

"Are we moving to New York?"

"That's not in the cards, sorry. But it looks like I am going to direct a play. Do you remember that strange party we went to on the breakwater, to watch the meteor shower, in the fog? Well, I met a woman there who teaches theatre at Connecticut College, and I proposed it, and it looks like it's going to happen. I'll have to get you a babysitter. I can't leave you here by yourself, you're not old enough, it would be too spooky."

"I don't need a babysitter."

"I know you don't, but it will be nice to have company."

David thought it would be more interesting for Joey to have a guy babysitter he could hang out with instead of another teenage girl. The long-haired boy he found, an ex-Marine, played video games with Joey and helped him with his homework and talked about guns. Gradually more of his life came with him, as he was there five evenings a week. Hour-long phone calls gave way to his girlfriend coming over. Joey was sent upstairs so they could make out on the sofa. Joey was cool, but when the phone bill came, the arrangement collapsed, and David took Joey with him to the last few rehearsals.

Nothing had been heard from Caruso for a while, apart from pecking and fluttering, and one bright Saturday morning David found the little bird lying dead on the floor of the cage. He stood there for a long time, then roused himself and called to Joey, who was getting the milk out of the refrigerator, "Look what happened."

"What?" Joey came in and saw. "Is he dead?"

"I'm sure he is," David said, reaching in and touching the body. When he picked it up and brought it out, Joey held out his hands for it.

"What happened?" the boy asked, holding the dead bird in his hands.

"I don'eet want to talk about it."

"He just died?"

"He didn't sing anymore. I must have forgotten about him. I forgot to give him food and water. I've been so caught up in the play. I feel just terrible." I rubbed against his legs, purring. "I won't forget you, Charles," he said. "Don't worry. Do you want some milk?" He went into the kitchen and poured me a saucer of milk, and squatted back on his heels while I drank it.

Joey had followed us. "I heard him chirping," he said. "Yesterday."

"So did I, but I didn't pay any attention. I'm

189

sorry. I'm sorry, Caruso. I'm sorry, Joey."

"Don't cry, Dad." Joey set the dead bird down—I no longer had the least interest in it—and put his arms around his father, and the two of them held each other close, patting each other on the back of the head.

•

Marco came for the opening of the play, driving up from the city with a friend. Bitsy was also coming, and David made dinner for them before the performance. Marco and his friend arrived while he was cooking. After greeting them with hugs and cheek pecks, David went back to chopping and stirring.

"How's the show going?"

"Fine, I think. We had a problem with the dimmers right up through dress rehearsal. The lights kept fading off a little very slowly and then fading back up in long loopy cycles. Apparently they had incompatible components. At first I thought I was imagining it, spacing out. I'm pretty exhausted. But it was definitely real. I thought the board operator was being creative, but he swore not. The system was doing it all by itself. They're bringing in a new board for tonight, I hope to God it's fixed. It was horrible. It was like energy

190

leaking out, and there was nothing you could do about it. Did you ever have that problem?"

"Oh, probably," Marco said. "I've had every possible problem." I had not seen Marco since I was very young, and he was older too, the wild-eyed young man now dapper and smart.

"Do you want a drink?"

"How about a joint?" Marco said, taking out a cigarette case and lighting a thin cigarette, which the three men passed around. Marco offered it to Joey, but David shook his head.

"Maybe you should go upstairs," he said.

"I'm O.K.," Joey said.

"What grade are you in?" Marco asked.

"Fifth."

"How is it?"

"Good."

"Do you have many friends?"

"Well, Eli and Abe, but we moved, and they're moving, so I have to say no, I don't. I am pretty busy. I play D&D on weekends. Do you know how to play Pong? I'll show you."

"Do you want to play your clarinet for them?" David asked.

"I'd rather not. Why don't you play the piano?"

"I'd rather not," David said. "I'm a little

stressed out."

"That's all right," Marco said.

"Do you have a harpsichord?" the friend asked.

"In the bedroom."

"Can I play it?"

"Sure. I'm afraid it's not in very good tune." The friend went in the other room and could be heard stumbling through a Bach Fugue.

"I'm glad you came. I wanted you to see this. I think it's good. You'll like the *mise en place*. I had to put this little play on a very big stage. I thought about it a lot and I think it works, it's like a room of light in front of an enormous backdrop. Curtains in midair. You'll see. Didn't you light this play in New York?"

"Yes."

"They're just kids, but they're talented. I know it's not the same, but I did what I would have done with anybody. You'll see. By the way, my sister's coming too. She should be here any minute."

"You must be joking."

"No, why?"

"I don't want to see her. I told you. I never want to see her again. I told you, the next time I see her I will throw her down the stairs."

"Marco, come on. What is this?"

"She is condescending. She is disrespectful. I don't need that."

"What are you talking about? She respects you. She knows how I feel about you, she wouldn't presume to have an attitude."

"I'm telling you how *I* feel. Fred, come on," Marco called, rising and putting his coat on. His friend stopped playing and came to the door. "We're going. Don't ask questions. I'll buy you dinner. We'll come to the play," he said to David. "We'll see you there. Just don't do that to me, all right? Come on, Fred." And they left, leaving David speechless in his apron, spoon in hand.

By the time Bitsy arrived rather breathless a few minutes later, he had made the table smaller, with three places set instead of five, and lit the candles.

"That took longer than I expected," she said.

He handed her a glass of wine. "We don't have very much time. I have to be there early to give the cast a pep talk."

"I thought Marco was coming."

"He's coming to the theatre, but I suggest you keep your distance. He's a little crazy, I don't know what he might do."

"He was always a little crazy."

"No, he wasn't. He's a beautiful person. He's just in a funny mood."

"He's a dope fiend. I am perfectly willing to be nice to him, but I'm not going to pretend I think he's good for you. Anyway I thought that was all over."

"It *is* over. We're friends. We're friends *again*. Friends are important. Never mind, just watch out, that's all I'm saying. Let's eat."

•

I liked having David home all the time. I liked to lounge around on the foot of the bed while he sat at his desk with his typewriter on a little table beside it, typing or at least thinking about typing for a few hours every day, breaking off to pace around or play the harpsichord or the piano or go for a walk. Joey, who had a paper route, came home after school to drop off his pack and then went back out with his paper bag to pick up his papers and take them around. The newspaper office was right next door, across a parking lot. I tried following him a couple of times, but he immediately had to cross a busy street I didn't want to mess with. The bag was big and heavy when he started out, and when the weather was bad sometimes David would take him around in the car. I went with them one time. Joey jumped out and ran up to put the paper on the porch or inside the door, and then jumped in and on to the next. He got completely wet, but at least he didn't have to lug the bag.

Alone, David slept under an electric blanket, which was too warm for me, so I usually crashed upstairs on Joey's bed. It all seemed a little temporary, frankly, but it was O.K., they were sweet together and getting on with life.

One weekend Joey was packed off to stay with the Schmidts and David went to New York again and I was left alone. Really alone, this time. He left me plenty of food and water but went off without even saying goodbye. He forgot, I guess. I was waiting on the piano bench. It made me feel like he didn't care about me. He had other relationships. I understand. But come on! I was simply furious. I thought about shitting on his bed, which would certainly get his attention if and when he came back, but that seemed a little beneath me at this point. I couldn't find any place in the whole apartment to settle down, even out on the porch, I was too mad.

So I left. It was raining, warmish, starting

to be spring. The drips from the roofs onto the gravel in the backyard were symphonic, the cars swishing by on the street beyond the parking lot like waves rolling up a beach. As I wandered through the old sheds and garages, dustier by the minute, my anger at David slipped away and my essential catness reasserted itself. It is tricky to live with humans, deeply wonderful, but too seductive, you can get *too* dependent and lose yourself. There are so many of them, and so oddly unpredictable. Essentially I am an anthropologist, not one of them but studying them.

As usual there was nothing of blood interest in the nearest buildings. I went on around to the other side of the big building, the newspaper, and found a cat way into the cellar. Knowing there was another cat around, I was excited and wary as I prowled the labyrinth of greasy rooms. There was no cat to be seen but there were mice everywhere! Enough thinking!

Maybe a whole day went by catching, playing with, killing, and eating mice, broken up with periods of sleep, until I couldn't manage another bite. I went upstairs in the dark and found the cat I expected in the doorway of a big room full of desks and chairs, arching his back, spiking his tail, hissing. If he wanted that to be his territory, fine. I went down to the far end of the hall and curled up and took a nap. When I woke up he had come out and was crouched down quite near me, making a low rumble. I looked at him mildly, and when he didn't do anything, I slowly and calmly got up, ambled over to him, and we touched noses. Nice.

In back of the buildings was a small wood on a low hill which proved to be full of more birds than I had ever seen before, little ones hopping about, which I could catch quite easily if I snuck up on them sneakily enough. It was a priceless opportunity to work on my stalking skills, and the rewards were beyond description. I saw David's car pull in, and I heard him and later Joey calling my name. After a while David came down into the parking lot looking for me. Later, after dark, they both came out, looking, calling, and walked clear around the block. I was still a little mad, and I was having too good a time playing at wildness, like him at the cabin; why should they go away and not me?

I stayed out for almost a week. By then I was lonesome. The red cat was a good pal, and the hunting was good, but I wanted more out of life.

David and Joey were happy to see me. David was reasonably cool about it, which I appreciated. I think he understood. He said he had been afraid I had been run over, but he walked around the block many times and never saw my poor smashed body in the road so he thought I was probably all right, and here I was. He sat down on the sofa, and I sat on his lap and licked his face, which made him laugh.

•

We had a visitor a couple of weeks later, a woman, whose name I gleaned was Margot. We were never formally introduced, but she noticed me right away and took my measure. She had a cat mentality, which said don't mess with me and I won't mess with you, but respectfully. I liked that about her. She was vivid, with long red and grey striped hair, dressed all in black once she took off her swirling purple cape. She and David were slightly overeager with each other, "turned on," I think the expression is. They cooked dinner together, and she made a point of being extremely nice to Joey, who ate it up.

David shut me out of the bedroom that night. At breakfast Joey asked his father, "Where did she sleep?"

"With me," David said.

They all three went off in the car, and Margot was not with them when they came back. There were a couple of other women around too that spring, but no love stuff with them, as far as I know. David's friend Victor came back from Maine for a weekend, and they got drunk and naked together on Saturday night and fooled around while Joey was off playing D&D, which seemed to be some kind of private joke. A certain restlessness was in the air.

•

"How is your novel coming?" Joey asked one night at dinner.

"It's finished, I think," David said. "It's a novella. A short novel. I don't know if it's any good."

"You always say that."

"Well it's true."

"What are you going to do now?"

"I don't know. I have to do something. I'm about to run out of money."

What is money again? Oh never mind.

I heard him on the phone a couple of days later saying, "Judith Malina has the idea that the city must have a lot of extra buildings and might turn one of them over to the Living Theatre, which as you know is an important theatre company and needs a place to perform. And since you are right there, I thought I would ask you. I hope you don't mind… Ah. Well, I'm not surprised, but I said I'd ask… Fine. I'm still in Rhode Island. Joey's here, he's eleven, he's in fifth grade… Writing a novella. I don't know what to do with it… As a matter of fact I do… Really?… Could I, do you think?… All right, I will. All right. Oh, that's exciting… Thank you."

As a result of this conversation, David lined up a new job in New York City, and that was the end of our temporary stability once again. He had to start almost immediately, and Joey had a few more weeks of school before summer vacation, when he was planning to go to his mommy out west. This created an awkward gap. David proposed that he stay with Beth and Rolf, who were ready to welcome him.

"Please, don't make me stay with them," Joey said dramatically, throwing himself down on his knees, pleading. "It's a fate worse than death."

"What's the matter with them?"

"Gretchen drives me crazy," Joey said, abandoning the dramatics and rising. "She follows me around and tries to kiss me. There is no peace. If I hide in my room she lies on the rug outside and scratches at the door and whispers my name. It's unbearable."

"She loves you."

"I love her. I love everyone. Just don't make me stay with them. Anything else would be better."

"I'll see what I can do. I hate to go off and leave you."

"Can't I come with you?"

"No, I don't have a place, I'm staying in a maid's room, and you have to go to school. Maybe you can stay with Jane Beall. Can you feed Charles?"

"Where does she live?"

"Three blocks, four blocks. You have to come by after school anyway to pick up your papers. Just come in and hang out with him for a little while so he doesn't get too lonely. I'm going to lock the cat door so he doesn't disappear again. You can come into the city on the weekends, or I'll come here."

This new adventure was fun for David, I expect, but it was not fun for Joey and me. I slept a lot. Joey fed me and played computer games for a while in the afternoon. One day he came in the morning and was there all day, skipping school.

Rolf and Beth came by and fed me when Joey went into the city for the weekend. Beth loved me up enough to hold me for quite a while. Joey spent his newspaper money on potato chips and ate so many that he started to get fat.

Chapter 13

Joey went west to his mother, and I went back to Rolf and Beth's for a while. I understood it was temporary this time so I treated it as a vacation or a house-guesting situation, enjoying the strange food and pampering. The grandma cat and I even had a romance of sorts, a kind of coulda-woulda flirtation, pleasantly stalled and oddly gratifying. The prima donna still snubbed me, strutting around haughtily; I didn't like her, but I had to admire her style and attitude. The kitten had grown up into an adorable young punk. I spent most of my time outside. Their overgrown backyard backed up on a disheveled inner block with a whole population of New England types. I observed without judging and carried myself with enough confidence by now that no one bothered me. Just to see if I could, I taught myself to catch moles, but why bother? There is not much meat on them and it tastes like dirt; mice have a much better flavor.

One day with no warning Rolf boxed me up and took me over to the old apartment, where I found David in the last stages of moving out. A medley of friends had gathered to carry the harpsichord and piano down the stairs and into the bed of a pickup truck. The piano was so heavy they had to slide it down; one of them had nearly been crushed bringing it up. There was something poignant about moving these heavy objects around. Cats don't have stuff.

We drove into the city and met another crew to help unload the truck. David carried me up first. I had no idea where we were going. We rose in a steel-box elevator, my first, then wobbled down endless brightly lit corridors with floors so shiny they made me dizzy. He keyed a door, we went into a narrow cluttered hall, and he called, "Hello, we're here."

He had moved in with Margot!

She was an artist, and this was the loft where she lived and worked. It had three rooms, high ceilings, big sunny windows with a view of the city and river and enormous sky. Unfortunately Margot already had a cat, Hortense, who from the first moment was implacably hostile to me, fiercely attacking me at every opportunity. Hortense was considerably older than I was and not terribly strong so I was not afraid of her, but I hate fighting. What was I supposed to do, bite her? It was her territory and it was not right of me to challenge it, I acknowledged that, but she refused to chill. The only place I was safe was under the bed. If I came out she was waiting and chased me back in. David fed me there, and I managed to sneak out to the cat box when I had to, pretty much. But it was a miserable life.

"What are we going to do about Charles?" Margot wondered one morning when David was getting ready to leave for work. He dressed up for his new job in a suit and tie.

"I don't know," he said.

"It's a problem."

"They'll figure it out."

"I don't think so," she said.

"They have to."

"It is making Hortense sick."

"She's the victim now? He can't even come out from under the bed."

"She is hardly eating anything, she is so tense and nervous."

"Why doesn't she leave him alone? What is the problem? There is plenty of room. She should get a life. I'm sorry, I am not giving up Charles. I can't. Charles is my closest friend."

"Hortense was born here. I am her mother."

"You knew I had a cat."

"And what are we going to do about your children?"

"I don't know. What are we going to do about anything? Play it by ear. I just got here, I don't know all the answers."

"That's a total cop-out."

"What is it, darling? Why are you attacking me? I am not your enemy." I knew just how he felt.

Soon after that my problem was cleanly and permanently solved when Hortense went to live with Margot's son, Jack. Margot held it against me at first, but gradually we warmed to each other. She was cat-friendly by nature and needed to ground herself by touching an animal every so often. She spent hours at a time standing at her easel with a paintbrush in her hand, and it calmed her if I periodically strolled through and rubbed against her ankles. I was glad to be there for her. She was taking good care of David, cooking for him, doing the love thing with him, giving him her desk so he could write and helping him move the furniture around. It was the least I could do.

I like apartment living. I like going outside too, of course, and I love to hunt. It makes my claws tingle just to think of it. But you know where you are in an apartment. It is all inside, all safe. There are a finite number of walls and rooms, caves and ledges, bright spots and shadows, paths and perspectives, coherent, comprehensible, limited, to be sure, but there are always limits unless you want to go into the wild, which I definitely don't. What you don't have any possibility of you don't miss. I was getting older, I had never been daring or adventurous, always preferring to be part of a family. This simple life suited me.

Margot had a teaching job at "Vassar" and was gone half the week, which simplified it even more. David worked nine to five and carried a beeper that unpredictably caused him to rush away even when he thought he was off. He was writing something too, grabbing fragments of time at his desk, playing sometimes the harpsichord, sometimes the piano. I liked to sit with him while he played, but I often slept most of the day away. I was tired of keeping up and gladly let months go by without trying to mark them.

•

Margot needed to get out of the city in the summer to focus on painting. She sublet her loft and rented a house in "West Nyack." David wanted his sons to come, singly or together.

"They shouldn't be separated," she said when they discussed it.

"Oh I don't think it matters that much," he said. "They're bonded. It is so much easier to pay attention to one than two, especially for a single parent. I'd like them to come visit this summer and then one of them stay on for school next year. Are you willing to do that?"

"It's necessary," she said. "They need their father."

"I know they do. Especially Joey, I think, but it's Sam's turn. He's a sweet boy. They both are. Are you seriously open to the possibility?"

"I wouldn't have brought it up otherwise. All I ask is that they stay out of my studio."

"You can close the door. How about they come for the summer and we'll see how it is? I'm sorry this is getting so complicated. I thought I could slip into your life without changing anything. That's a laugh. We'd have to give them our room."

"You can build us a new room at the other end."

"I'm not that much of a carpenter."

"You built your cabin. You've built harpsichords. You can do it."

"You're right. I can do anything. At least I

used to think I could."

"I'll help you."

When David called Doreen and talked it over, it turned out that she was eager to have a year off so she could go to graduate school. So Margot had her way and the two boys would come to stay. Joey had been enrolled at a private school, thanks to his grandfather; Sam would go to P. S. 41.

First we went to "the country," where the break-in period was rough. The house had a big yard surrounded by suburban wilderness: I'd be fine. Joey and Sam came to vacation with their father. David commuted into the city to work a forty-hour week. Margot wanted to paint all day; instead she had two energetic boys to contend with, from the time she dropped David off at the station at 7:15 until they picked him up ten or twelve hours later. The long hot evenings were heavenly in the secluded yard. They put up a net and we played badminton until it got too dark for them to see. I didn't really play, I'm kidding, apart from grabbing the "bird" a few times and running off with it, just to surprise them. I loved watching them leap around laughing.

Margot didn't usually join in. She was sick of

the boys by the time David got home and went upstairs with a book after dinner. Many nights she brought him back out into the yard after the children were in bed to tell him how miserable she was.

"What am I supposed to do?" he said. He flopped down on the grass as she paced around him in the shadows.

"You can't imagine what it's like. I'm one of those suburban moms and they're not even my children."

"I know it's hard."

"It's not hard for you."

"It is. It's surreal. It's all I can do to stay sane. I step onto the train and turn into an unsympathetic character in a movie I would never want to see. We get off *en masse* and flock over to the Hudson tube, a train like some relic of Dickensian London. It's a total time warp under the river. Once we clank and squeal into the station I am swept along in a river of people flowing up twelve parallel escalators in the basement of the World Trade Center, which land us in an Alphaville shopping mall, where we scurry off in all directions. It's a good walk to City Hall so I arrive sweaty. Work is not unentertaining, but it's not exactly my thing,

210

you know. I come home from that insanity and immediately have to generate a few hours of fun. I mean, they're kids, it's summer vacation, they're supposed to be having fun. I like to have fun too. But I'm pretty well used up by then. So I'd really rather not get up out of bed in the middle of the night and analyze our feelings or whatever we're doing."

"I haven't seen you all day. I need to talk to you."

"We can talk in bed."

"They'll hear us."

"So what? We're only human. I'd rather make love."

This went on for some time. I walked away from it, scratching at the screen door and mewing till one of them let me in, and went to sleep in my chair. They eventually went up and all was still.

The boys started going to day camp and then Margot had her days free, which was not enough but better. As soon as she came back from the morning taxiing we settled down in the living room, where she had set up her easel and paints, and she painted steadily all day until she had to go pick people up, scrutinizing a stalk of some plant she had stuck into a bottle, dipping her tiny brush in different colors and carefully applying them to her small canvas. She set me up in a comfortable chair right beside her so I could watch, as if I had any sense at all of what she was doing. I didn't, but it was sweet to be close.

Uncle John, David's cousin, was there for the Fourth of July bringing model airplanes and fireworks, which scared me half to death. Joey won a camp medal for archery, and Sam announced that he had learned to swim. Margot finished two or three small paintings, and David seemed to be surviving, even happy sometimes. Thus weeks went by.

"What are we going to do when day camp is over?" Margot asked him one night when it was too hot to sleep. I'd gone out with them and we were lying on a blanket on the grass in the moonlight.

"I'll think of something," he said.

"No, you won't. You'll leave it till the last minute, and then I will have to eat it. Obviously I can't say no. I won't do it, take care of them yourself."

"No, you'd rather suffer so you can beat up on me later."

"You son of a bitch."

"No really, please, I'm doing the best I can, it doesn't do any good to complain. Sam can go visit his friend Jeremy Smart in Mystic. They like him a lot, I'm sure they'd be glad to have him, I'll call them tomorrow. I am thinking of sending Joey up to the Catskills to help Marco light a play. It's time for him to learn something about lights. They can both stay away for a week. Then I'll take a week off and we'll go up to the cabin. How does that sound?"

"You trust Marco? You don't think he might...?"

"I do, yes. Do you think I shouldn't?"

"I don't want to go to the cabin. I feel superfluous. Trapped. You really only want to be with them."

"Of course I want to be with them, they're my children. But I want to be with you too. I wish you would come."

"I have to work."

"You can paint up there."

"I'm in the middle of something here."

"Whatever."

"I hate that expression."

"So do I. I will never say it again. Do whatever you want, that's what I meant to say."

One evening as they were about to sit down to dinner a car drove into the driveway and honked. "There's Marco," David said. "Are you ready?"

Joey ran up the stairs. I followed David out onto the porch. It was raining heavily. He ran out and got into the car. After a while the horn honked again, Joey ran out with a duffel bag, and David hurried back to the house.

Margot came out on the porch as they were driving off. "Why didn't you invite him in? I made plenty."

"I know. I did. He wants to get there before dark. Anyway he had somebody with him, to drive." He was wet.

"You don't want him to see me."

"That's not it at all. You don't want to see him anyway. You don't like people to be gay."

"They don't notice that I exist," she said.

"How can you say that? Half your friends are gay."

"They really have no use for me, though. I am under no illusions. They would rather live in a world without women. Marco doesn't even say hello to me. It is inexcusably rude."

"Don't be silly."

"My feelings are not silly."

"No, of course not, that's not what I meant, but I do think you could rise above whatever this is, paranoia or homophobia. You liked *me* when I was gay, maybe better than you do now."

"Do you wish you were still gay?"

"No, I don't. I like gay people but I don't want to have sex with them. I only want to have sex with you. How can you imagine I'm gay? If I was gay why would I be sleeping with you?"

"I don't trust you."

"Now now. I beg you." He tried to put his arms around her but she pulled away. "Are you having your period by any chance?"

Sam appeared in the door. "I'm hungry," he said. "Let's eat."

•

David took Sam away to stay with his friend and came back and we had a quiet week sans children. On the weekend David and Margot went away in the car to see the play Joey was supposedly working on. Marco, it turned out, had had a paranoid fit and left his driver and Joey stranded in a house in the woods for most of the week with nothing to do but play Monopoly while he set up the lights himself. David went on and on about how great the play was.

I stayed with Margot while David and the boys went up to the cabin and realized how much I had been yearning for an extended period of peace and quiet. She painted all day. Nothing happened. I loved it. I thought I could happily go on that way indefinitely, but of course I was his cat, not hers, and the guys came back, smelling of wood smoke, and soon after that we packed up and moved back into the city. I was ready. Nature is great when you are young, but later on I have to say security is more important. I never had been a bold explorer of the great outdoors, and now I tended to feel exposed, even hunted, if I wandered far. Margot's loft was plenty big enough for me.

David retrieved the boys' bunk beds from storage in Connecticut. He and Margot moved their bed to the far end of the living room, and David built walls to screen it with built-in bookshelves and a sliding Japanese door. Margot was a passionate cook; the little family had dinner together every night around the round table. School started, and David walked the boys to school every morning on his way to work. There were kids of all ages in other apartments on other floors; Joey and Sam could go out to play without leaving the building. Margot started teaching again and was only home on weekends, which made it hard for her to paint, which made her edgy. There was no place for David to put his desk except up on a platform at the side of her studio, which made her feel invaded even after he erected a half-wall to separate them. The steep ship's ladder was a scramble, but I liked being up there as he cozily shuffled papers around and typed on his new computer.

Joey at fourteen was seriously involved with this computer, which had been configured to his specifications, and he too had to come into Margot's studio to use it, which she pointed out to David was contrary to their original agreement. He said he couldn't put the computer in the boys' room because he wanted to be able to write on it, he needed a work space too, and besides they couldn't even see her at the easel, and anyway she was very seldom there painting. She hated the very idea of it even so and as a result was permanently mad at David, saying he was the enemy of her work, although other times they were harmonious, crazy about art together, and had many friends who came over and had fun. Margot was helpful and positive with the boys, but a dark gray cloud could often be seen hovering over her head. Many nights there were tense scenes at the grownups' bedtime, which I did my best to get out of the way of. At worst they escalated into furious denunciations, chases from room to room, door-slammings, and throwing of things by Margot, once a full pot of hot rhubarb.

The emotional climate was wildly variable; they were either very very good or unbearably horrid, and meanwhile the boys were growing up, which was enough. The sunmer between the first and second years they staayed in the city and David rebuilt the boys' room, carving it up into three separate spaces, Joey's up above, Sam's over by the window, with a tv cave for the family tucked cozily under Joey's floor. The piano, which had been taking up most of the truncated living room, was trundled up to a friend's apartment on a higher floor, and Sam, who was taking lessons, went there to practice. David went back to the harpsichord—which I preferred, although I seemed to have heard all the pieces before. Sometimes two ladies came over and played recorders with him

I gradually lost track of the details of these

busy lives; at some point I realized I had given up paying attention. It had become all I could do to keep myself reasonably together. I couldn't think about other, separate beings, who swirled around me like scenery or dreams. I figured I was going senile and doddled about feebly. I could no longer manage the ladder up to David's study; he carried me up with him and plopped me down under the lamp on his desk while he read or scribbled or played with his penis or typed on his computer. I blissed out.

•

Sam went back to his mom for sixth grade, and Joey started high school. David made him a lunch the night before and got up and gave him breakfast before sending him off at seven every morning. His new school was in "the Bronx," an hour on the subway. Margot's new teaching job was even farther away and she was gone for weeks on end.

That fall David lost his job—something about an election, which his guy lost—and went to work for Marco, who owned a lighting business only a few blocks away and needed help, despite Margot's fierce disapproval.

"I don't know what else to do," he said. "I

need a job, and he needs me. I don't have some other job offer I'm turning down, you know."

"It's a drug business," she said. "What kind of an example are you setting for your sons?"

"No it isn't," he said. "It's completely separate. It's not even in the same place. There are no drugs there. It's a lighting business. I love lighting, as you know, or should know."

"You just want to be with Marco."

"I *do* want to be with Marco, but I'm working, believe me. I wouldn't be there if somebody didn't have to be and I wasn't being paid."

"I wish you didn't have to work on Saturdays."

"So do I, but he's the boss. I wish I didn't have to start so early in the morning. He's not a very pleasant boss. He's not well. It's hard for all of us." Marco came for tea one time when Margot was away looking shrunken and pale.

I don't know how much time went by before they realized that I too was seriously ill and took me to the doctor, who poked and probed me and found I had a blockage of some kind. Twice a day for weeks after that Margot gave me medicine up the butt, which was surely not pleasant for her. David, who had been doing meditation again, seemed passive or even fatalistic about the whole thing, Buddhistically unattached to the outcome, and I could see the virtue in that: I'd had a long enough life, more varied than many cats', and David was doing all right now. I wished he was happier with his work and got along better with his lady-love, but I'd done my best. He knew I loved him.

Margot, however, was not prepared to let me go and took me to the hospital, where I had surgery, after which I was so miserable and weak that I thought I was going to die. Everything seemed to be falling apart around me too. I heard quarrels, and making up, angry words, weeping. Margot's brother died; I heard their sorrow. Marco died; I heard David telling Joey. Joey was not there much, and then gone altogether. David's father died; I heard him tell Margot. He went away and came back. I had withdrawn into my own misery, but then very slowly realized that I was actually starting to feel better than I had in a long time. She had saved my life.

Chapter 14

We moved again, another marathon drive, just David and me in the truck this time. The dreaded box was consigned to the trash. I didn't feel much like moving around, but I enjoyed being free, and I was cool with road trips now. I liked the sense that something else could happen.

After some days we arrived in "Denver" and stopped to visit the little theatre I remembered from so long ago. David carried me into the building, cradled in his arms, and up the stairs to the apartment and dance studio on the third floor. It was like going back in time. Was it real then or now? Was it a stage set? He embraced his loved ones, who were older but still the same, and they had a drink and a visit, and then we were off again. Do other places exist when we are not there? It had never occurred to me.

After more miles we stopped in New Mexico to see Joey and Sam and Doreen. I had never expected to see her again. She was living in a comfortable village adobe with a new lady-love, Oralia, who was a veterinarian, of all things. Doreen was excited about the fish pond she was building out front, which made my mouth water, but there were no fish as yet.

Doreen thought I was too thin. Oralia laid out newspapers on the kitchen table and thoroughly examined me. I was taken aback but decided to give in.

"He's all right," she said, after poking me all over and peering into my eyes and ears and mouth. "How old is he? Eighteen?"

"Joey is seventeen so Charles is probably nineteen," Doreen said.

"He's very old," Oralia said, "but he is in good shape. He's still enjoying life. Aren't you, Charlie?" she said to me, rubbing me below the ear. I'm a sucker for that stuff.

"He was sick for a long time," David said.

"Well, he's better now. I don't think you have anything to worry about."

What a nice person!

David took Sam out for a ride on Doreen's motorcycle. I was alarmed when they loudly wobbled off down the drive but they came back after a while happy and invigorated.

"That was rad, Pop," Sam said as he slid off the back.

"I liked it too," David said, switching off. "It's fun."

A little later Joey, who was living on his own in a different town, showed up driving a rackety old pickup.

"Aren't you supposed to have somebody with you on a learner's permit?" Oralia said.

"I'm almost eighteen," he said. "They're not going to stop me in the daytime."

"We'll have dinner early," Doreen said.

"I know what I'm doing," Joey said.

"I'm not suggesting you don't," Oralia said.

"Let's go for a walk," David said. "We'll be back." He put his arm around Joey's shoulders as they walked down the dusty road and out of sight. I stretched out in a patch of sunlight on a flat stone beside the pool, dreaming of fish.

We spent one night there. I was not sorry to go. New Mexico is beautiful but the winters are wicked. I didn't want to live there again. I don't want to be cold anymore. I was delighted when our trip ended back in sunny Santa Barbara.

David stored his stuff in an empty garage, and for a while we lived in a room in a house with a dog, which was large and shaggy but benign. David kept me shut up in our room at first. I could hear the dog snuffling outside the door. He was just curious, he didn't seem to mind me. I saw him eye-to-eye a couple of times as the door opened and shut, just sitting there looking at me, and the next day I asked David to let me out. There was no problem. The dog was an older gentleman like myself and we became good pals.

David set up his harpsichord in the dining room and had the house to himself all day when the owner was at work. But clearly this was not our house. He needed more space around him, a bedmate, a workroom. I knew him.

The next move took us to a place I had never fully experienced: suburbia. David moved in with a new amour named Catherine. I had met her two or three times when she came over and they did the love thing in his room. She was a tall, decisive woman with a soft spot for cats and for David. She cuddled me and he cuddled her, all of us purring in our different ways. Catherine had a spacious house of her own with a large backyard full of California-type plants. We slid into her life and house without any great fuss, afloat on an underlying harmony quite different from the more turbulent vibes with Margot or Doreen—or Marco, for that matter. There was eager conversation, music, and frequent love stuff. It was intoxicating to be part of it. Plus there were no other animals in residence. I could relax.

Sam immediately came to live with us and started going to high school. David had left his piano behind but Catherine had a better one, long and black. They played it together, sitting side by side on the bench, kissing at the end of a piece. Catherine hosted meetings in the big living room, fifteen or twenty people sitting around in a circle of chairs talking earnestly, figuring out another move of some kind. Ultimately David and Catherine decided they liked the house they had, and the meetings ended. Her three grown-up children came for short visits at long intervals. David's mother came over for lunch on certain occasions, at first walking with a cane, later in a wheelchair, avoiding any interaction with me. Catherine's father came sometimes with a rolling oxygen tank. Everyone was well behaved and cheerful.

Life was not as funny as it used to be, but I say thank heavens. I was ready to settle down.

•

How am I going to tell you about my death? Well I can't, obviously. So I will just take you up to the moment of it, and that will have to be the end of my tale.

I was ready. My own issues were long ago resolved, and David was happy with Catherine. That was a lucky break.

"Let's have a family reunion," David said, "your family, my family, get the generations together while the old ones are still with us. What do you think?"

"I love it," Catherine said.

"I know where to start but I don't know where to stop. Children, obviously, and their children, if any. And how about our children's other parents, ex-spouses, ex-spouses' new spouses? Shouldn't we include them? It would be fun to have everybody together."

"Will they want to come?"

"Doreen will, I think. We're very friendly on the phone. I like Oralia. They are perfect for each other, just like us. It's amazing how it all worked out."

"Margot?"

"Margot doesn't want to see me or even hear from me."

"How do you feel about that?"

"It's just the way she is. How do you feel about Hiram?"

"He is greatly improved. I always liked him,

just not his attitude toward women. He is better with Sally, she wouldn't put up with it. And I'm much better off with you."

"So?"

"Let's do it."

That was the second winter. I was stiff and couldn't keep warm, even though it was sunny and mild, nothing like winter in New England or New Mexico. I could go outside when I felt up to it and walk a little on the garden paths. The garden was pretty in that dry prickly desert way: I prefer a moister, greener, softer landscape, but I suppose the balminess makes up for it. There were holes in the fences but I didn't want to go anyplace. Raccoons prowled around at night. Generally I preferred to stay in, lie in a patch of sunlight, and gaze out through the big glass doors.

The chief drawback of Catherine's house was the slick white glazed tile floors in the main rooms. I was never sure of my footing on them, plus they were cold. So imagine my pleasure when a crew came in and chiseled them up, making a hideous mess for days, and put down a beautiful new wood floor, dark, satiny, and warm. Maybe they didn't do it for me—maybe they did.

The big family party happened at the end of June and lasted several days. Joey came from New Mexico in his truck and crashed in Sam's room; the two guys went out after everyone was asleep and came back in the wee hours. Others flew in. Catherine's older daughter and her little girl were in the guest room. Other visitors went elsewhere to sleep but came over for breakfast and hung around. There were people coming and going all day, Doreen and Oralia, Catherine's first husband and his second wife, Catherine's other children. The aged grandparents came one afternoon for a formal feast. The old man tried to talk to the old woman, but she was too deaf and vague. I sat on the sofa—David had to lift me up—and most of the people I knew came over and spent some time with me.

The next day everybody was going for a picnic in the mountains. There was a great flurry of activity after breakfast. I was sitting in the bedroom hall, right outside David's writing room. I knew I was in the way but I didn't seem to be able to go any further. I was afraid somebody would step on me but nobody did. Joey and Sam went back and forth carefully stepping over me.

Gradually the house quieted. I heard car doors slamming. In the distance I heard Joey say, "Is Charles all right?"

Oralia came and knelt down beside me. My eyes were not focusing. She gently pulled back my eyelid.

"Shall I bring him some water?" David said.

"You could."

Doreen hovered in the doorway. "Do we need to do something?"

"No," Oralia said, stroking my bony back. "He's fine."

"He's had a long life."

David came with a saucer of water, knelt down, and held it under my nose. I tried to drink a little of it, to show him I appreciated the thought.

He set the saucer close by. "Shall I stay with him?"

"No, you should go," Oralia said.

"Yes, come," Doreen said.

"He wants you to go. He wants to be alone. We'll wait for you."

The others went away quietly leaving just me and David, on his knees. He leaned over and put his face close to my head and breathed on me, his hand very lightly stroking my back. Say

230

something, I thought. But I guess he couldn't. We understood each other. We both knew that. He struggled to his feet and left, locking the outside door behind him. "Here I come," I heard him say, then car doors, and cars driving off.

The house was still. I was comfortable, composed, my paws crossed the way David likes.

I bowed my head.